FORWARD

Welcome to 12+1 Tall Tales of Imagination. I would like to take a moment to thank you for purchasing this copy of my first collection of short stories. Here within these pages you will fall down the rabbit hole of imagination, you will be taken on a journey of fear, horror, panic, disgust, joy, sorrow, pain, torment and all the other sweet emotions which I hope to lay at your feet. I make no apology for any of the books content as the title states it is only imagination here not reality, so my only DISCLAIMER is….

If you are easily offended by subjects containing, horror, torture, death, murder, religion, hate, lust, sex, fear or damnation of souls. Then please read no further, close the book and hide it away in a dark damp place and forget about it, however DO tell all of your family and friends how awesome the book was and to rush out and to purchase a copy straight away.

Still here? Good lets continue...

12+1 Tall Tales is a collection of 13 short stories, these are just a few which I have written of the last 30 or so years but they are the first to be published. The stories subjects are diverse as I wished to cover a wide spectrum of my imagination. You will take a glimpse into my dark mind with stories such as 1916, here we find ourselves thrust deep inside the First World War fighting for our lives in a battle we little understand, yet one which holds great fear and terror.

THE ALLEYWAY takes us on a journey of sexual deprivation and twists our understanding of the order of the world. FREAKSHOW reminds us that sometimes we only see the things we want to see and not the reality that sits in front of us. DESECRATION sledgehammers our belief in religion; it forces us to question the words of others in our understanding of life and death. This still remains one of my favourite short stories; I still get Goosebumps whenever I read it. Even old Saint Nick makes an appearance in SANTA. We are shown another side of the afterlife in SUICIDE, one where things are not what we think. SHOPPING LIST teaches us to be care full what we wish for. REBIRTH lets us taste our own mortality. HOMELESS shows us the world we will never see constrained to our normal lives. FRANK AND TONY well you'll simply have to read that one for yourself. THE

BAND takes us to a dark world of pain and fear; it lets us guess if that world could really exist. HELLBURP was written many years ago following an experience I had very similar to this.

Ill finish by saying that I hope you enjoy these stories as much as I did writing them, I'm sure there will be more to follow now that I have tasted the sweet rotting meat of these printed words, their smell of fetid moulding pages and now I have swam in the sea of all your horror filled souls...... ENJOY

CONTENTS

DESECRATION

REBIRTH

HOMELESS

FRANK AND TONY

THE ALLEWAY

SANTA

1916

HELLBURP

FREAKSHOW

SUICIDE

THE BAND

SHOPPING LIST

37

Desecration

The stone sailed through the air, lazily tumbling over and over it rolled, its surface rough and course, weathered over millions of years by time itself. Small cracks littered its outer crust. Deep in the bowels of mother earth immense heat and pressure birthed this weapon. Its only purpose to wait, to sit on the craggy ground through millennia in solitude for this moment. Picked up by the hand of its destiny from amongst hundreds of other likewise rocks it was plucked. Lifted towards the heavens grasped tightly in a shaking hand, then swiftly launched at the enemy.

I was that enemy.

I never saw the rock travelling towards me, like so many others I only felt its impact, but this one. This one felt different, I felt the hatred which lived within the throwers heart, I felt the hatred and also I felt her fear, fear of something unknown, fear of fear itself. In that moment of the rock hitting my face, that moment that it's craggy surface bit into my flesh and tore it open I lived her life through the rent in my face, I saw her life, her love, her fears, I saw her sorrow and her joy, and I felt her pain and wore it inside of me. As the blood replaced my tears I looked into her eyes, into her soul and forgave her, instantly she became aware of my love filling her body, embracing her soul, taking away her fears and replacing them with light. Slowly, nervously her lips, twitching replaced her grimace with a smile, a smile of love and of understanding.

I felt every stone, every rock which was hurled at me in hate, Each one giving me a small glimpses into the throwers fear, each one opening up a fresh wound upon my body, yet with each jagged impact, with each ounce of blood which I spilt I became stronger, I became invigorated, my soul lifted. I knew that my body was ravaged by the torment it was suffering, the stones, the rocks, the wounds and open flesh, the false crown of thorns which pierced my skin and grated against bone. All of this and so much more which my flesh has endured. But still my heart sang praise, praise to these beings who knew not what they do. My will like my soul carried high on warm winds, energy, love, understanding, compassion, light, all flowed through me, lifting me, allowing me to walk, to stagger forward even with the weight of the rough wooden cross held over my torn shoulder I was able to stride towards my destiny.

I stumble and fall to my knees, the hard rocky ground cutting deep, the cross slamming into the crown, a thorn snapping against bone, a finger braking against the hard ground, then my breath rushing from my lungs as the flail digs deeply into my weeping back, the sharp talons ripping free pieces of my flesh and hurling them amongst the baying crowd. I must rise, I must stand and continue my journey, I cannot fail them. Father give me the strength I need to help them, let me not fail them or you my father.

Through the crowd someone pushes their way forward, he kneels down before me dressed in rags not even sandals on his feet, he is holding a small wooden cup filled with tepid water , with head bowed he offers the wooden chalice to me like the starving might beg for a piece of bread.

With a hand twisted and broken I reach out and touch his hand and drink from the cup, the water is cool, refreshing, soothing but tastes of my blood. Raising my bloodied eyes I look into his face and see the tears streaming down it, in that moment, in that glance I show him all. He becomes a king amongst kings, his soul becomes pure, his heart will live forever, his love will encompass all. His eyes tell of his understanding. In that instant, that moment we sit and understand a lifetime, we simply be in that moment for ever. Even when my centurion guard kicks his hand away and pushes him swiftly back into the crowd his eyes glimmer with the knowledge of love and light.

Slowly, painfully I rise, my body screams in protest, my muscles refusing to move, my heart beating strong, my flesh weakening, my blood spilling, my love flowing. With a jerk I manage to will my legs to move, slowly I place one shattered foot down upon the stony ground, then the other, my back bent with the weight of the wooden cross, it cuts into my muscles, splinters pierce my flesh, the thorns in my crown grind and scrape. Please father just a little further, give me your strength, your love and your mercy.

Ahead just away a small hill is set before me, on each side they stand, stand and watch, some still throwing rocks, most, most now are silent, watching with lowered heads, understanding slowly tightening its grip. My breath is ragged, my lungs burn as I stumble forward, not fast enough for the guards as they flail me again and again, each time tearing away my skin, I beg for the pain to stop but I know that I must feel it, I must suffer the tearing and spilling of my body, I must take in the torment, let it devour me so that I may cast it out.

Father, father I ask you to be by my side, to walk with me as I walk this tortured path, I ask for forgiveness, forgiveness for these souls whom know not the injustices that they do against you. Please father give my body your strength so that it may suffer the pains of their sins, let my blood wash over their souls and cleanse their light. Father, father why do you abandon me in my time of need, am I not your son ?. Have I not pleased you with my offer of my flesh for their sins ?. Your silence disturbs me father. My time has almost come to an end here on this mortal earth farther , am I not to join you in the heavens and walk amongst the everlasting light at your side. Please father I beg of you bless them with your love and understanding.

I stagger forward, each new step brings with it a new meaning of pain, each breath brings fresh waves of suffering, it washes over me in torrents', I'm drowning in my own suffering and my father still does not answer my pleas of mercy.

　I reach the crest of the hill, here it flattens off to a small plateau, my legs can bear me no longer and I collapse to the ground, the wooden cross landing heavily upon my rent back, hitting my bloodied crown jarring a thorn into my skull, the pain forces me to cry out in silent pain and anguish, why has my father not answered me?

　As I feel the cross being lifted off me, it pulls away a strip of flesh which has become snagged in its rough surface. Slowly, as slowly is all that my destroyed body can do now, I raise my head slightly and look to my left, then to my right. Either side of me laying prone as I am there are two other bodies, one on each side of me a few feet away. They too have suffered the same fate as I have; their bodies lay battered, beaten, torn and molested. Their injustice was to steal bread in order to eat. Their crosses to have been taken away and laid upon the rough ground not ten feet in front of us. I can hear their ragged breaths, lungs almost collapsed as is mine, all around there is stillness, no sounds or voices, no wind, no birds, just absolute silence. I know that this is simply my body slowly shutting down, dying of the abuse it has suffered, I close my swollen eyes to pray to my father once more but before I can I'm roughly lifted by strong weathered hands under each arm, partly lifted but mostly dragged I'm turned over and dropped onto my back. My head slams into the cross beneath me opening a fresh wound and driving the thorns deeper, pure white light fills me and for a moment I think it is my father, has he come to rest at his sons side, to cup my soul and bath away the savaged wounds, but alas no the white light is merely a new dimension of pain, my entire soul now feels pain as a bright light. Looking up at the clouded sky I silently call for my father...father....father....

The soft white clouds sleepily drift across the heavens, their passage never ending, their softness never comforting, their moistness never quenching.

I slowly drift in and out of consciousness as my mind struggles to hold onto its sanity, I know this has to be done, this has to be endured, this is my destiny,. My gift to them my sacrifice for them, my blood spilt for them, my love for them, my life for them so that they may live. Words have no meaning, no strength or volume of the love which my heart holds for these beings, they who are capable of so much. Little do they know of their potential, of the good in themselves, of the love and light which they hold.

My minds drifting is violently cut short by the hammering in of the first iron nail through my hand, fresh pain explodes through my mind, spittle flies from my split and swollen lips as I scream, the first, and only sound which I have uttered since all of this molestation has begun, I will not utter another sound I must not, even as the long nail is driven through my broken hand and deep into the cross, it grates through flesh, through muscle and through bone shattering the few remaining shards of my

hand. Only when its head is flat against my palm do they stop, with weakened sight I look up at the face of my torturer. He crosses to my other side with the second nail and heavy bloodied hammer at the ready, yet just before he begins to drive in the nail he glances into my eyes, in that moment I see his pain, his regret at what he must do, I see his torment lived until his last breath, the torture of living this moment again and again for eternity. This is his fate, this is his destiny, one which he is summoned to perform, one which he is commanded to do.
   And I forgive him……

   In a moments glance he understands that he is forgiven all, his torment, his torture of these memories are all forgiven in that instant, and in that instant of recognition, that spark of understanding he looks to me and smiles, even as he hammers the second nail into my flesh he smiles. My vision darkens my mind screams for mercy, my soul cries a river of bloody tears over the land forever and I hear my father's voice, like an angel softly treading through the clouds I hear his whisper, it envelops me, wraps me in its warmth, I feel my torment fade, my pain subsiding, my rent body relaxes in his whisper, I spend an eternity in his light and his love, my soul transported to another plane of love, I can see my body far below me in another time, another dimension, I see how ravaged its flesh has become, the broken bones, the torn flesh, the blood flowing free, my hands are spread wide, nailed to the cross with long wrought nails. I see the crowd stood forming a large circle watching, waiting, waiting for the end to come, I long for it also, my body, my mind willing the end forward, wanting the torment and suffering to stop, for there to be an end to my desecration .my breaking mind begs my father to release me...

And he speaks..

"my son. Does thou love me?"

His words are like a rainbow, it fills my heart with awe to hear them spoken, like smiles from a baby to its mother his words quench the fires in my soul,

"yes father, I love thee, my soul hold thee in its pastured light,"

I answer yet not with words that man uses, my answer comes from within my soul, unspoken yet carried upon angels wings.

"father, father do I not please you, have I not pleased you by my offer to you of my body, they know so little and understand even less father, I have taught them your word showed them the true path to your light and love, but father please let it end my body is broken, my flesh ravaged, is it not symbol enough for them, do they not now know your word, please father let me sit at your side once more so I may bath in your glory forever."

Delivered upon the wings of angels his answer kisses my bloodied face.

"It is nearly at an end my son." he answers

   His presences leaves me, he is gone, I'm left alone to face my end, his words fill me with rivers of love, his light fades but remains at the corners of my vision. The warm embrace relaxes, I feel my pains return, I am back, I am here, I am me, my twisted body screams at my mind, I cough blood which snakes its way down my face. As if to enforce my return to my shattered body the third and final nail is driven through both my feet, white hot pains smashes through my mind, I hear the bone splinter, I hear...

   My father has retuned all my senses to me, the end is close and I must feel it all, I must hear it all, I must see and smell it all. He has given me these gifts so I may bear witness to my end. Thank you father.. You truly are great and mighty..

   To either side of me the crosses have been raised, I never heard their cries as the nails were driven through the flesh, each man now hangs by their own body, each taking turn to scream in agony as the nails tear slowly through the flesh, its progress only being stopped by bone. Their time has come to pass, their bodies are not of this world any longer, their trespasses will be forgiven by my father if only they were to ask, ask for his forgiveness.

   With a heave my cross slowly rises, men pull upon ropes as others push with their backs, sweat forms upon their skin even though the air is still. As I'm lifted higher and higher my feet and hands begin to take my weight, I feel the iron nails tearing skin, ripping flesh and muscle, grating bone, the blood flows as though it to wants end to my torture. I am raised almost vertical and for a fleeting moment think that I am going to topple forward crashing to the ground when suddenly, jarringly the cross drops a full four feet into its post hole, the sudden impact jolting my whole body downwards, I almost scream my agony as my right hand is almost torn completely through, my feet twist almost to the point of braking my ankles.

Please father I beg of you end it…..

We, the three condemned hang from our crosses as our charges are read aloud to the crowd. It's strange. Where once there was cries of hate, volleys of malice thrown at me now there only remains silence. A slight breeze has begun, it lifts up the silence like leaves and scatters it all around. All are stood frozen in place, still as summer corn with no breeze, each woman, man and child stood frozen, watching, waiting, wanting, hoping that an end will take us soon, finish our suffering, begin the new era, start afresh in the knowledge that the son has returned to his father's side, his sacrifice accepted, his blood spilt in his father's name restored, his body, ravaged and destroyed once again restored. All waiting. All except one.

I look down with dying eyes into the still crowd and see him, slowly walking amongst them, unseen by others, unheard or felt. He is looking straight at me, straight into me, he is looking into my soul His eyes are black like the robes he wears, his face is a face of many, he wears their souls upon his face, its surface ever changing ever twisting and contorting into the next but I know him, I see him and I know him, he knows that he cannot hide his true face from me, I see him behind the many faces and I see him grinning, his mouth twisted and perverse, his teeth long and sharp like the fangs of a cobra, his skin shimmers in the sunlight like the scales of a snake, his forked tongue flicks from this foul mouth, and slithers to and fro, dripping black slim. He watches, watches and waits, he always waits, he is always there waiting, feeding, destroying. His soul blackened by the souls of those he has taken, taken with false promises false hopes and dreams, feted words of comfort and of love. He watches me now knowing my end has come, waiting, waiting to taste the souls of those who accept his lies, to feast upon their light and to gorge upon their rotting corpses. Slowly he weaves in and out as he waits never taking his eyes off me, wanting to taste my soul and I know him…..

   The guard lifts his spear high, draws it back with a well-practiced stroke, one born of battle and thrusts deeply, its sharp point penetrating my ribs on my right hand side, easily it slips deeper and deeper pushing apart ribs as it goes, one snaps another fractures and pierces my lung, still he pushes further and further until at last he reaches my heart, this is my end, destiny has taken me here, I'm going home to my father, my lambs will live forever in the light of the almighty. The spears tip enters my heart and begins my homeward journey. With only peace, love and light in my soul I look down to forgive the guard for his trespass and look into the black eyes of my father, his fork tongue licks his sharpened teeth with anticipation, his grin widens in feted joy as he knows I'm coming home..

I love you father, I'm coming home………..

THE END

REBIRTH

It begins with darkness, a thick visceral darkness like no other.

Softly muted sound penetrates the blackness, a melody, an illusion of notes and words being entwined. Being created, woven together in union. The vibrations moving the very air, each molecule swaying to its own dance.

My consciousness becoming in an instant, protons collided, electrons fired and in that instant I became. I am.

I know this melody, these notes, these cords, and these words even. My mind screaming as it claws and scrape's its way back into this world. My cognitive mind lurches as it starts to move, much like the screaming motion a steam train makes as it sets forward on its journey. It's the music, the melody; it has brought me back, back from where I do not know, my mind swims like a thick broth. I cannot recall who I am or where I am, I don't know how I recognize the music, and I simply know that I do. I cannot recall any past memories for I don't recall what a memory even is.

The soft muffled voice of the singer sooths me like a loving mother, my mind settles letting me know I am here, wherever here is. I have no senses apart from hearing, I feel nothing, no taste no scent no touch, no whisper of presence. Gaining any one of these would shatter my mind, I know yet... I have no sight just blackness. I don't even know if I have a body just a mind existing in a void of black emptiness.

My mind focuses upon the music and its song, the words sound so far away, so distant yet so familiar, I know each one by heart, each syllable. A picture of the holder of the words flashes in my mind like a strobe light. I can see him in my mind's eye, his face his skin, every pore, every detail. I know him, I know his name. Michael Stripe. It echoes through the caverns of my mind, his name is Michael Stripe. He is singing the song, the song I know from far away, from another time, another age. His velvet cords plucking at my mind, like unseen caresses the words enfold my soul. 'Well, everybody hurts sometimes everybody cries '

There, it happened exactly then, with just those six words my mind became unshackled, in an explosion of freedom everything came back, my mind instantaneously being uploaded with everything that I am, was and ever will be, in that millisecond of cosmic time I regained every knowledge I ever had and it shattered my soul.

I'm dead.

My name is Leston Potter, I am 39 years old, I lived with my wife Stacey and our seven year old daughter Jessica, 37 rows road Huddersfield uk.

But I am dead.

My last memory was of my wife sobbing as my heart finally gave out, I suffered a massive heart attack at home late one evening, the ambulance had come and the paramedics had worked on me for twenty minutes, I was awake the whole time. I knew that my time had come to pass over, I felt no pain just love, my soul had been embraced by pure love, I had watched as my body of this earth had been given up, my wife crying and pleading for them to do something, to not give up. And I had been at peace, light had filled my heart and I had left, but now, now I was here in this darkness, I still had no feeling in my body but as the music continued I knew that I was laid on my back, my head felt rested, I moved my eyes around in their socket but could not penetrate the blackness. Like hurtling bullets the thoughts flew through my mind, what am I doing here, am I dead, did I survive the heart attack, why is that music being played and why is it so muffled.

I had a thought of movement rather than a sense, my mind felt as though my body was moving forward, slowly this was justified as the sound of the music seemed to move slowly further away, then slowly it disappeared altogether leaving me in total darkness and void of any sound at all. My mind began to panic, running through every kind of scenario that it could, could I be dreaming this ? Am I in a coma?

  Heat, heat can be defined as 'the quality of being hot, high temperature

Well now I could feel heat, heat coming from all sides, the strange thing was that I couldn't feel my body but I could feel the heats energy upon me. Slowly it increased, the temperature rising up and up, my mind frozen like an old movie on pause. The heats ferocity building, my body absorbing it more and more, the feeling of it edging in to my mind little by little. Then at the far away edges of my mind there came light, tiny miniscule flickers of a wispy vapour at first, then slowly eating its way further and further in to consciousness until finally it began to enter my vision, small specks at first, tiny specks of dust it swam at my sights edges but growing, ever growing, beginning to light my blackened void. All the while the heat relentlessly growing, my body beginning to slowly experience the sensation of burning. Is this hell? Am I burning in hell my mind screamed piercing it slumber.

  As the light grew and my vision restored I could begin to make out shapes directly above me, with each passing second both heat and light worked as one, together as symbiotic lovers they weaved their works. I willed my vision to clear, screamed with my soul to clear the fog from my eyes and when it did I wished that I had failed.

   Directly above me no closer than five or six inches was what looked like a silk fabric, looking left and right using only my eyes I could see this fabric returning down at my side roughly ten inches at each side. Then, then I knew, I knew that I was burning, the flames licked up and around my body, I saw them as they danced and pranced around my shoulders, I felt their hot caresses, their burning embrace. I knew, I knew that I was in a coffin and that I was being cremated. My mind, no my soul knew that I had died that day but here I was unable to move or scream, stuck, forced to feel every flame which played at my skin, forced to endure this horror and unable to stop it, unable to yell and shout, unable to make it stop. My only thought was that I was about to face hell, my melting flesh charring, sizzling and popping as the fire consumed me. My mind, my soul begging for the pain to stop, begging whoever was listening to release me from this hell, take my rent body, cast my soul down into the fiery depths of hell but please I beg you stop this torture. Even as my face became taught then slowly began to blister then melt I begged, why.. Why can't my mind close down and save itself from this? Have I done so much wrong that I deserve to suffer so…

And then as though my screams of mercy were being answered a bright white light wrapped itself around me, cleansing me of all suffering and pain, stripping away my mortal body. I could feel its warmth, its coolness, I felt pure white love, I felt joy like I had when I was a boy in the arms of my mother, I felt the kiss of god upon my forehead, I heard the voices of angels as they sang to my soul and slowly my vision darkened, it narrowed to a pinprick far away in the distance and I stayed there in that womb of heaven for an eternity, just cocooned in love staring at the pin of light.

Then slowly after eons the light grew closer, closer, closer. Like a lazy day beginning it slowly began to fill my vision, it enveloped me, guided me, brighter and brighter it grew until I thought it would blind me. And then I heard it

'Come on now Sarah one more push I can see the baby's head '

My soul shed a tear as everything that I was, all that I had been ceased to exist my body reborn, my soul refreshed.

With a cry I entered this new world...

THE END

HOMELESS

From out of the darkness there came light.

Slowly, softly at first the light began to filter through his closed eye lids. Probing, prodding, and fingering his retinas, seeking out the darkness of his body and mind. The sun raising its rays warming as it signalled the birth of a new day.

The prone stranger lifted a hand covered in a lifetimes worth of grime and shielded his eyes from the strong sun's rays, using his other arm he slowly lifted his body up into a sitting position. The damp cardboard which had been used as a make shift shelter to cover his sleeping body during the night was now discarded and tossed away to the side of the large metal skip.

The skip stank, the cardboard stank, the floor stank and most of all the stranger stank, not a small stink, not a stink like a week old t-shirt worn out in the sun's heat lifting heavy timber 10 hours a day. This stink was a stink all to itself, it was a sweet tangy stink, kind of like rotting chickens skin that's been left on the side of a barbeque grill, when the weather turns suddenly and we all run indoors for shelter, leaving the skin to sit and fester as its forgotten about till the next bbq, whenever that happens.

This stink came from years of neglect, a lifetime of clothes and skin unwashed, grime so ground in that it became a part of the persons DNA. This stink, this ordure couldn't be washed or cleaned away with soap and detergent. This stink was like a fingerprint, each one unique to the owner, so unique in fact that each and every other homeless person who had spent any length of time on the streets could tell each other simply by the stink, like a pheromone name tag each one wore their identity tag proud, the vapour always announcing their arrival several feet in front.

The stranger lowered his grimy hand and scratched at his birds nest like beard, the sun now softly caressing his stained face, embracing his body with warmth and whispering delicate promises of far off places of warmth and plenty.

The funny thing was he couldn't really remember bedding down here, in fact the harder he tried to think about how he had gotten here the more he realised that he had no memory at all, none until waking a few moments ago.

For a long time he simply sat and thought, letting the sun's rays wash over his body. But no matter how hard he tried he simply couldn't remember anything, not a single thing before he had woken this morning,

Not his name, his age, how he had gotten here, where he had come from, where he was headed to, nothing.

Running his hands through his dark greasy shoulder length hair he let out a long shaky breath, his stomach grumbled and churned. Letting him know one thing at least, it was hungry.

Rising from the rough ground he searched around looking for any clue that might trigger his memory, the skip at his side was open so he reached in and rummaged around looking for his breakfast, hoping that maybe a little food might do the trick.

Well it was not a full English breakfast but the half chewed big mac would have to do, ok the bread had a little mould on it but what the hell I suppose you could say it had penicillin as a bonus. He took a large bite and began to chew, instantly spitting the mouthful back into the skip. Well at least he remembered one thing, he hated gherkins. Peeling back the remaining top bread roll he picked out a small slice of gherkin and threw it on the ground then replaced the top and devoured the whole thing in one.

Suddenly a large car came screeching out of nowhere hurtling towards the stranger, its driver fighting desperately with the steering wheel to try and regain control. One of its rear tyres had suddenly blown out sending it into a wild spin, in her panic the driver had stamped on the accelerator pedal and jammed her running shoe between it and the centre panel. The car bucked wildly as she fought to control it narrowly missing an oncoming lorry.

The stranger reacted faster than he had thought to; he hopped from foot to foot like a premier league goal keeper before throwing himself to the left seconds before the car sped through the very air space which he only a heartbeat ago had occupied.

The car thrust forward crashing head on with the skip, instantly its bonnet crumpling like an empty drinks can, the skip being pushed back fully six feet with the impact, both front tyres blew out and the rear of the car lifting three feet into the air before smashing back down to the floor and blowing out the remaining rear tyre. The sound of the impact and the metal as it twisted and crumpled was like symphony being conducted in a breakers yard. Bits of metal and broken glass were thrown all around like deadly BBs from a hand grenade.

The impact was so violent that the driver was hurled through the windscreen, like a rag doll her body twisted and smashed its way out through the screen, like a javelin the unconscious driver was thrown forward only stopping when her face met the skips front panel, with a sickening wet thud her face kissed the cold hard steel, milliseconds later her body folding in behind it, almost cartoon like her shattered form slid down the steel and thumped to the floor, it lay there twisted, legs splayed arms disjointed, not quite looking right, the posture was wrong somehow, it looked kind of jumbled.

Rising from the rough ground the stranger stood and surveyed the carnage before him all had gone silent, deadly silent. Not a sound was made, not a bird singing nor a dog barking, nothing just an empty void where there should be sound. He felt numb, not cold but just numb. Slowly in his mind the clouds began to lift, he saw himself stood in front of a large lake, the water flat and still, a fine mist caressed the water's edge, he knew this place it was...

Before he could grasp the memory his body jolted as though an electrical shock had passed through him, instantly he was back here in the now, in the present stood looking at the horrific scene before him, instantly he knew what he had to do, his body reacting, his mind commanding. Swiftly he closed the gap between the driver's prone body and his own, in two strides he was at her side. Then something took over him, he didn't think what to do he simply did what he must do, his body moved and made motion without him telling his brain what to do. The instructions were already given, his muscles already obeying.

Kneeling on the rough ground the stranger reached out and took hold of the drivers left leg, slowly and with practised ease he carefully laid out the leg straight on the ground, then her right leg, again with flow of unknown certainty he straightened it next to the left. She had luckily hit the ground on her back so he didn't have to turn her over, her smashed face was turned away from him but he knew it would be pulverised from the impact. Next came her arms, each broken appendage laid out at her side, the hands laid flat and some of the fingers unwound from each other. Finally to the head. Holding his breath the stranger reached down and slowly turned the drivers shattered face towards himself.

The jaw had been completely shattered, one eye had been torn out and the other had popped, its empty clear sack sitting on her cheek still attached by the optic nerve. A fist size dent in her forehead indicated the point of impact.

Bile bit at the stranger's throat eager to spew from his lips. He swallowed hard and steeled himself against the sight in front of him. Then without thought or reasoning he began what he knew he must do.

Placing both hands at the top of the drivers left thigh he slowly ran them down her leg, applying no pressure simply sliding both hands down over the thigh, the knee, the shin and on to the foot. Miraculously the leg straightened behind his hands, the compound fracture closed, the bone retreating back inside, the skin sealing, healing. The foot realigning itself, the torn skin closing.

Next was the right leg, again the same healing and mending of bone, skin, and ligament. Like some kind of magic worker the stranger moved his hands over the driver's body, mending, repairing, making whole what had been shattered. Finally he moved to her face placing his healing hands over her forehead and slowly moving down, like some Hollywood movie affect her head, her face, her body became whole again, became new, healed, restored, alive. With his work complete he simply stood, turned and walked away from the skip, the mangled car and the driver, the now living breathing driver.

Sirens screamed behind him, the ambulance racing to the scene, its paramedics jumping out and running to the driver's aid. The first paramedic feeling a strong pulse and the driver beginning to wake up, turning the paramedic watched as the homeless bum shuffled away pushing an old rusty shopping trolley as he went. Lazily the bum looked back then turned his head skyward, smiled and spoke soflty in a whisper to the skys.

One at a time a father, one at a time…………..

THE END

FRANK AND TONY

With a loud plop a big fat rain drop fell onto Frank's head, it had been raining all day and the skies still looked like bloated balls of cotton, slowly the light had begun its endless fade to darkness.

"I just can't do this anymore Tony" Frank said in a gravelly voice.

Turning to his lifelong friend Tony, Frank shook his head at the exact same time another fat droplet bounced off, wetting his already soaked face.

"Come on Frank, you've had slumps before. Remember that time when your home got squished by the developer's? I know things are bad at the moment bud, but Darlene and the kid's need you man. Think of them bud, how are they going to continue if you're not there?" Tony wiped away a droplet which was lazily rolling its way down his head.

Frank turned his gaze forward, he looked out across the busy motorway that stretched out in front of the two old friends, out beyond the cold hard tarmac surface the bright lights of the city had begun their nightly dance, each giving everything it had to outdo the next, each hoping to shine the brightest, each glowing the hottest, like luminescent plankton floating on the oceans current the lights twinkled in their dance of light and luminance. Frank hated the foul smelling city with all of its hustle and bustle, he hated the speed of the cars, the constant noise, he hated most of all the people with their ravenous appetite for progress, always building, always thrusting forward, always advancing their futures on the backs of the little ones.

"They are all that I can think about Tony, it's because of them that I find myself here, I can't take care of them any better than I can take care of myself my friend. Darlene knows I can't do this anymore pal, I know she has been seeing someone else, I'm not blind. All those times she's just hopping out or visiting family, yeh right. Just how much of a fool does she think I am? No I'm telling you Tony it's the only way out for me." Franks eyes glazed over as he moved closer to his friend.

Whoosh, the air rushed against them as a large lorry thundered past, steeling himself from its blast Frank looked out again at the lights off in the distance. Right now he longed to be home, home with his loving wife, where he should be, not out here in this foul weather. But he knew it was his only option, his whole life had led to this moment, Frank knew in his heart he had no other way out, no matter how hard his best friend argued, his path was set.

"Come on Frank, don't do this bud. You got everything to live for, this aint the way out pal. Damn it Frank I love you bud." Tony blinked back tears

Frank looked back at Tony. " Yeh I know you do pal, you love me so much that you have taken care of Darlene for me for the past seven months."

Tony's mouth dropped open.

"Oh I know Tony, I know all about you and my wife. I've know from day one. You and her like kids, running off at any opportunity and you know what gets me the most, the lies. Why not just come out and admit the affair pal, some best friend hey."

Frank looked over at Tony's ashen face and continued. "I know you got feelings for her bud, hell you always did. That's why I'm asking you to take care of her for me when I'm gone, I can't stop the two of you getting it on together so just do the the favour of staying with her, her and the kids. Can you at least do me that one thing bud?"

Without looking at his best friend Tony slowly nodded, he had no words; he never wanted this to happen it just kind of did. He always knew that Frank would find out some day and he was ok with that he loved Darlene, he swore to himself he'd do it, for his pal he'd do it.

Without hesitation and before his friend Tony could even react Frank leapt forward out onto the wet slick road. Instantly a hurtling trucks headlights caught him freezing him in time, time which played at half speed as the oncoming trucks front tire thundered over Frank. In a millisecond his tiny green body was squashed as flat as piece of paper killing him instantly. Just another common toad killed on the endless road of life.

THE END

THE ALLEYWAY

Relentlessly the rain fell, its cold wet spear like droplets smashing down onto the hard tarmac and shattering into a million diamonds. Darkness had beaten the downpour by over an hour, it masked the rain in a cloak of blackness. The alleyway through which Rachel walked more resembled a small stream or bubbling brook than the inner-city back ways which it was.

The alleyway stretched ahead, its only light coming from two dim street lamps, one at either end of the fifty-yard stretch. Like any other alleyway this one was littered with the discarded flotsam and jetsam of city life, packing crates, empty containers and several over full Wheeley bins littering its narrow corridor. The shops and fast-food outlets using it as their dumping ground until ordered by the city to remove the waste, which happened less and less frequently. It became the playing ground for the ever-increasing number of rats which made the city their home, their numbers out growing its human population. Their physical size increasing each year as they feasted upon the wanton waste of the city dwellers, who in their greed and gluttony discarded banquets of food, the rats literally living like kings and queens off of the unspoilt waste.

Rachel hugged her coat tighter around herself as a cold chill blew its best to open it. From behind her a discarded bottle clattered along the ground, the sound amplified in the narrow confines of the alleyway. Quickening her pace, she dared a quick glance over her shoulder, nothing. Just the relentless bloody rain. Christ, she hated the rain, its cold embrace teasing her exposed flesh, its icy kiss wetting her cheek, she felt its chill in the pit of her stomach.

Ahead the lamp flickered threatening to plunge her path into total darkness, but on the third or fourth flicker it found a fresh thrust of life and resumed its mournful glow. Then Without warning the lamp exited life, instantly Rachels path fell into darkness, her steps faltered as her eyesight rapidly adjusted, from behind came a sound which drove a stake into her heart.

Footsteps

As if from nowhere the steps were directly behind her, no gradual approach, no gentle build to their sound, these steps just happened, Rachels heart stopped, her mind raced, her pulse froze, the rain fell and then it happened.

A strong hard hand took hold of Rachels shoulder and spun her fully 180 degrees, the speed and force barley giving her head time to follow, her shoulder bag being flung off to her side hitting a discarded food crate. Her mind screamed for her to react, to do something but the attacker still gripping her shoulder struck out with the back of their other hand, its speed thrusting rain droplets before it. The impact striking Rachels cheek deforming her face and snapping her head to the side, before her body could react another blow was swiftly dealt, this time to her stomach. The blow being sent with the intent to fold her double and fold her it did, Rachel doubled over as her breath rushed from her lungs, her arms uselessly flailing as she dropped to her knees. She felt the grip on her shoulder release as she fought with her body to gain control and take a breath, her head swam in a sea of white hot stars, time had somehow been slowed down, through her blurry vision she could see each and every rain drop as it glistened on its downward journey, sound had somehow been turned down to simply a low buzz.

Through her dream state of consciousness, she felt her face being roughly turned skyward, a dark and brooding figure stood over her, its shadowy form cast against a dark background of pain. The strong hands squeezed her face into a pucker and far off in a distant place she felt herself being kissed. The attackers lips warm and wet, their mouth open, breath fetid and their tongue probing, searching out her mouth's interior. The tongue slithering and sliding, working its way between her own lips, its tip seeking the depths of her mouth, her on tongue working in response against her attackers; for a split moment in the fractured passing of time Rachael was taken from the alleyway, she became transported to a moment from way ago in her passed when she had felt such exquisite delights of carnal lust with her then long time lover. Her mind embracing the memory, her body reacting as its eroticisms took hold, despite the current situation she felt her nipples harden and her sex become moist. For too long she had not felt this kind of a sexual excitement.

   As rapidly as a flame is spent Rachael's reminiscing was abruptly cut short, the hand which delt the fierce slap to her face was driven by something other than love or lust, its soft texture a stark contrast to its hard purposeful intent. Her head snapped to the side, instantly deep red finger welts formed on its surface, a small dribble of blood formed in the corner of Racheal's mouth threatening to trickle down her face. The attacker followed up the blow with a reverse one which held just as much hate at the first.

   Racheal's head swam, the blows had almost knocked her unconscious, only her panic kept her from embracing the warm creeping blackness. Still kneeling on the wet littered alleyway, she braced herself for another onslaught of blows, raising her arms up Infront of her face she hoped to protect herself from the attacker. Seconds became minutes, minutes became hours, hours became a lifetime. Then from some far off corner of her senses her mind began to speak to her, slowly in a child's whisper it told her the attacker was moving, they had stepped away from her and slowly had walked round to her rear, her mind whispered a sonnet of verse letting her know that now was time for action, now would be her only opportunity of escape, now was the moment to act, now was the time to run..

Grasping the thought tightly in her mind Racheal fuelled her muscles and thrust herself upwards springing to her feet she exploded into motion; and so to did the attacker. As though they had a looking glass into her mind they knew her move even before she had. With a force only gained through years of dedication the attacker swung a devastating blow to Racheal's right kidney.

For Rachael the blow felt like a sledgehammer being ploughed into her, an explosion of pain accompanied a searing white light, her mind imploded and her vision tunnelled, her breath had long left the building. Like an unloved scarecrow she crumpled back to the floor, on her hands and knees she bent double desperately trying to suck in a much needed breath. Racheal felt that with her outwardly blasted breath had gone all hope, her attacker was simply to strong and too fast for her to fight or escape, she felt her only course now was to breath and survive. Suddenly her back became somehow heavy, pressing her knees and hands deeper into the filth and sludge of the alleyway floor, from over her right shoulder she felt hot stale breath on her ear, her mind raced.

Using their weight to pin Racheal down the attacker used her moments of disorientation to their advantage. Dropping to their knees they quickly reached round and gripped Racheal's throat in a large strong hand, slowly squeezing, tightening, gripping. Applying just enough pressure to slow her blood flow, not enough to stop it and cause her to blackout, but just enough to drive home the message of compliance. Using their free hand the attacker swiftly reached down and began to unfasten the buckle holding Racheal's coat closed, with a sharp tug the buckle gave allowing free access to her shirt and trousers, as with the coat buckle these gave very little resistance.

   For Rachael it all became about survival, she knew that fighting would only get her beaten or worse, she knew even without her mind having to inform her that the only option left was to endure what was about to come, but most important was to survive it. Her mind closed down, her emotions switched off, her soul took itself away to another time and place, her body became a hollow vessel as she submitted to the impending violation. All that was left to Racheal now was to feel, to feel the tugs and tares as her shirt was ripped open, to feel as a strong cold hand grasped each breast roughly squeezing each hard-protruding nipple in turn. She felt, felt as the cold strong hand ran its course down her stomach and on to the band of her trousers, the eager forceful tugging as the band gave way. Rachael could feel that her attacker was male, repulsively she could feel his hard-erect penis pushing against her rear.

   Grasping both trousers and underwear in one the attacker swiftly pulled them down over Racheal's hips and rump exposing her bare flesh to the icy rain. With his breath quickening the attacker fumbled with his own trouser zip, he ripped the zip downward in a manic effort to free his manhood. His veins coursed with adrenaline, his mouth felt dry and his throat felt course, his erect penis glistened as the cold night embraced it. He felt so alive, so in control of his own destiny, he felt all powerful and invincible. He truly was the master of all, the god amongst gods, this mere mortal beneath him would never know how truly magnificent he really was. It was his right as a god to take that which he desired, that which belonged to him and so he did.

Rachael could feel herself becoming wet despite the ferocity of the attack, she could feel the attacker's stiff penis pushing against her rump, she felt it twitch and throb against her and in some way, it excited her, her already erect nipples stiffened further. Closing her eyes, she submitted her body to the impending assault.

Using his own legs as leverage the attacker forced Rachael's own legs further apart, reaching down he grasped hold of his pulsing member and slowly stroked its glistening tip upward then down along the crack of Racheal's rump leaving behind a wet silvery trail of fluid, his breath no more than a whisper he steadied himself in readiness for the thrust which made Racheal spit out a gasp. In one fluid motion the attacker thrust his hips forward, released his grip on his manhood and entered Racheal's sex only stopping once his stomach had slapped against her rear. He felt Rachael's sex embrace him tightly, felt her own wetness as it greedily sucked him deeper in, hearing her gasp only heightened his experience.

   Rachael could feel the attacker slowly stroking his thing against her sex lips and anus, its heat and wetness. Her mind longed for him to enter her, to slip slowly inside and fill her whole. Suddenly without warning the attacker did just that, he thrust forward gliding his member between her lips, she gasped as he entered and continued to thrust forward; he felt large, easily filling her sex. Forward he thrust only stopping when she felt his hips contact her rump, Rachael was glad as she thought that she couldn't have taken anymore of his pulsing cock. For what felt like an age he teasingly remained buried deep inside her before slowly, achingly slowly pulling back, inch by erotic inch he withdrew his manhood, almost completely but not quite, he left just the head of his cock, now glistening with both his and Rachael's wetness, inside, just enough to swell her outer lips slightly apart allowing just a small coolness of the night to caress her.

   Caught up in the raw animalistic moment of it all Rachael wanted more, she wanted to feel him filling her again, to feel him filling her again and again, without thinking it she pushed back with her rump forcing the attackers ridged cock back deep inside herself, she felt him respond with another thrust, this time more forceful and urgent, this time his thrusts zenith was met by a loud slap of their combining bodies. Without a moment's hesitation he fully withdrew then speared her sex, again and again, he withdrew and speared each time gaining a new level of urgency. His thrusts had become fast, hard, almost primordial in their attack of Rachael's body. With his head held back he faced the dark skies as the rain fell soaking his features, like a wild boar he grunted with each new thrust, like talons his finger dug deep into Racheal's rump.

Rachael's mind swam in a sea of euphoria as her whole body responded to the ecstasy which coursed through it, she meet each new raging thrust with an equal wanton backwards thrust, her sex pulsed her breasts slapped to and FRO, her body demanded more, more, more. From deep inside she could feel the birthing of an orgasm, its beginnings forming at the pit of her sex then rapidly gaining body, swelling growing, expanding, nothing could be done now to stop it and stop it she did not want to do, her head became light, light as a feather, small beads of perspiration formed on her curled back lips of her mouth. The pleasure overtaking her body, working her mind into a frenzy until it could take no more. In an explosion of light her orgasm gripped through her, Rachael's whole body convulsed as it tore through her; her sex gripping tightly the thick cock buried deep inside as her breath exploded from her lungs. At that moment of ecstasy her body had become a trigger, her sex becoming the vessel for the attacker's own emergence from the light, as the orgasm tore through Rachael it triggered his own eruption. In a moment of religious decadence he felt his heart pause a beat, felt his cock swell in size, felt his scrotum contract and his body begin to convulse as he came inside Rachael, for what felt like an eternity he felt himself emptying his seed into her, like a river flowing to the sea he continued to twitch until at last he was empty.

Stepping around Rachael he zipped his fly's back up, reaching into his pocket he pulled out two fifty-pound notes and tossed them down onto the sodden floor in front of her.

Lifting her head Rachael looked from the discarded money up to the shadowed face of the attacker, her own face now carried a red hand shaped welt.

"I've told you before not to touch the face "Rachael spoke through clenched teeth still a little breathless.

Father Daimen retrieved his white clergy collar from his inside pocket and slipped it back into place.

"my child you are paid to do the lords work, so take the money and don't be late next month. Oh, and may god bless you my child "Grinning he turn and disappeared into the shadows.

THE END

SANTA

   The full moon sat high in the night sky, its light glistened on the fresh snow which covered the flat roof, it twinkled like a million diamonds, each reflecting the pure white light. Then It began, with a gentle tingle of energy, in a small space just above the roof the night sky sort of blinked, pulsed almost. Tiny flecks of light blinked into life, they flashed on then off then on again before slowly starting to spin, faster and faster they spun, their light growing brighter and brighter, faster and faster, brighter and brighter they grew, the air turning, twisting, churning faster and faster,until all of a sudden, they spun as one, a solid spinning light around 8 feet in diameter, its light so bright it hurt to look at. Then quick as a flash the light exploded and vanished leaving behind a figure, tall as a post and round as a barrel.

The soft white snow crunched beneath his thickly soled boots, the night was still, not a sound could be heard. His breath billowed from his lips like smoke in the crisp nights air; his big round belly shook as he walked; grasping hold of the thick leather reins Santa climbed aboard the brightly decorated sleigh; its wooden running boards creaking beneath his ample weight. Taking his seat, he turned to his brightly dressed elf helper and grinned mischievously,

"Well stitch that's the last one, all four billion gifts delivered, another year's work is done, I do believe we are ahead of schedule this year. I guess it's time we head on back, what you think?" he asked.

"yeh. Let's get going." stitch said forcing a finger up one nostril, the first knuckle disappeared up the snotty orifice quickly followed by the second.

Santa reached out and slapped stiches hand away from his face forcing his stumpy digit back out and bringing with it a long slimy bogger. It stretched and stretched between his finger and nostril like a string of goo. In one swift sweep stitch flicked his hand out wrapping the snot around his finger before deftly popping it into his mouth like a lolly pop. With a lip-smacking pop, he drew out his finger all clean and shiny.

"That's disgusting stitch, hope it tasted good." Santa asked with a smirk upon his face.

"Delicious" stitch answered licking his lips.

'guup' Santa shouted as he gave a whip to the reins. With a jolt all eight reindeer heaved pulling the sleigh forward, accelerating faster and faster; by the time that they had reached the roofs end both they and the sleigh were no more than a blur. Santas hat threatened to fly off his head as the wind whooshed by, snitch sank down a little and cwatched in a little closer to Santa.

With another crack of the reins Santa pulled them back flying the sleigh up higher and higher into the crisp night, the reindeer's hooves moving so fast that a path of sparks were being left behind. like a firework they flew faster and faster.

"come on boys you can do better than that, now mush mush you scabby lot." he shouted.

From down at his side Santa lifted a large long whip, its thick leather wrappings covered in gunge and blood, its end knotted and covered in sharp hooks. In a well-practised throw of his arm and a twist of his wrist he sent the whips end flying out over the flanks of his reindeer, reaching the end of its arc and with a loud crack it pulled taught, the talloned end digging deeply into the rear of blitsen. The reindeer howled in pain as Santa pulled the whip back, the sharp ragged hooks tearing deeply, ripping flesh free and opening up the hide. With a deep booming laugh Santa flick his wrist again sending the whip out over the reindeer, again hooking more flesh, more hide, this time Donna paid the price of flesh. This continued as the sleigh rode higher and higher, the reindeer howling louder and louder, Santa laughing harder and harder and the hooks sinking deeper and deeper. Even stitch manically laughed as he frantically dug out more snot.

Higher and higher and higher until they became perfectly silhouetted by the full moon they rose, then pulling with all his might on the left reins Santa halted their rise. The reindeer sharply turning, twisting, thundering back down towards the earth, each glad for a respite from the whip pulling harder and harder, faster and faster. Their speed increasing even further.

"let's go home stitch. Our work is done. I'd love to see those little faces when their toys fail, their bikes break and their dolls all rot. Come on my beasts take us home". Shouted Santa.

Faster and faster, they plummeted towards the earth, the friction from the air began to burn the sleigh, the reindeers hides catching flames, their howls becoming screams of agony, all the while Santa cackled and grinned, even as his own flesh began to blister and burn, he laughed. Stitch lazily gazed at his own burning arm, watching impassively as the skin fell away, the flesh slowly cooking before being burnt black then it to dropping away. In the blink of an eye Santa had become transformed to a burning, screaming skeleton, his white fleshless fingers grasping the reins, his body reduced to maggot filled hollows; his eyes long melted away to be replaced by two flaming red orbs, their centres a dark obsidian black, a pronged snake like tongue darted forth licking rapidly at his sharp fang like teeth.

   From below the ground swirled round and round, its rocky surface began to spin as though caught in a twister, round and round, its centre falling away, falling down, down into nothingness just a black bottomless void; its edges ringed with leaping fierce flames. The pathway to hell invitingly, longingly yearned to be entered by its master, it called with a million screaming voices, each burning deep with the tortures from hell. Like a lover waiting to be entered the void longed, its soul laid bare.

   With a hell spawned scream, one born of a ten thousand lifetimes of pain, sorrow and suffering Santa, stitch and the remainders all disappeared into the void, it devoured them in one gigantic swallow, closing with a loud deffening thud leaving behind nothing but a soggy mount of chared soil. with a belch hell burped throwing out a final spurt of heat, flame and rank stale air. a hidious soul reaping cackle accompanied the burp...

THE END

1916

"Shit... Shit... Shit."

   This is it, its happening; I'm really going over this time. My heart is pounding my blood is racing through my veins, I'm sweating buckets and I can't stop shaking. I'm gripping my Enfield .303 so tightly that my knuckles have turned white. I'm breathing fast, my breath clouding in front of my face in the early morning mist. I wish I was back home, back home lying in a warm bed listening to the rain pitter patter on the window pain. Instead I'm here in this cold wet trench, I'm freezing cold, my uniform is sodden through, I've not had any food in two days only a few crackers to eat and some stale water to drink. God I wish I was back home, back home where mother could hold me tight whilst telling me that things would be alright. Instead I'm here in this bloody trench, surrounded by the smell of death and decay, there are bodies slowly rotting not ten feet away from me, they have been there for the past four days ever since the poor sods were cut down by the bloody German Mauser which has me pinned here now.

   The trench I'm in has partly filled with water, doesn't it ever stop raining in this hell hole, where ever this hole is, I can't even say the name of the place I'm in, I know it's in

France but that's all I was told, don't help when I can't read the names of the towns, I wish I had listened in the school my mother sent me to more, I wish I was back there, I wish I was back anywhere, anywhere but here. I'm going over and I can't stop it, I know I'll end up like those poor sods ten feet away, everyone who has gone over has never returned, that bloody mauser...clack ...clack..clack..clack.. All day it goes, why can't they run out of ammo, why don't they stop and go away, I don't want to go over, I don't want to die, I don't want to end up like those poor sods ten feet away. Cut down, hell cut in half by the mauser with its 7.92mm bullets ripping through my flesh killing me till I'm dead, dead, dead...I wish I was back home.

   The mist is slowly starting to lift, the skies are slowly lightening, the clouds are slowly passing over, and it may stop raining. Bloody great, now I've got to go over it might stop raining., .everything is wet, soaked through by the constant rain, the trench is like a muddy stream knee deep with thick brown muddy water, an oily film sits on top shining with iridescent colors, the sides of the trench are veined by the constant water running down them, even the rats have deserted me, scurrying away to find new rotting flesh to chew on...

   My mind drifts back to the day I enlisted, to how excited I was and nervous all at the same time, excited that I would get my chance to see the world, to travel far and wide, to see the sights that I had only heard about, excited by the thought that I would get my chance to kill those krouts, to get my revenge for them killing my papa , somewhere in France my mother had said, some cold wet bloody field, she said he had been cut down by a German mauser hidden in a fox hole, whatever a fox hole is...bastards I'll get them, I'll kill them for you papa...scared that the enrolment sergeant would find out that I was only 14 and not 16 like it said on the letter of consent which I handed him, a letter which Reggie my best friend had penned for me, his handwriting so neat and well versed that the sergeant never gave me a second glance. That same day I was taken to a waiting ship and transported over to France, I never saw my mother before I left, it all happened to fast. I hope she doesn't take it too hard, Reggie promised me that he would go straight round and tell her that I was going to get those bastards back, back for my papa. I wish I could see her now, hold her tight tell her that I'm sorry, tell her that I won't be coming home, that I have to go over and there's no one else left here in this water logged trench but me, tell her that I'm going to meet papa, cut down by a German mauser just like papa, I wish I could tell her not to cry.....

   I'm violently brought back to the present by a mortar shell exploding not fifty feet off to my left, it sends fist sized balls of mud flying in all directions, some hit me with surprising force. I throw my face into the mud and curl into a fetal position, tears stream down my face as I weep. All I can think is that if there is a hell then I'm in it.

   Even with the explosion still ringing in my ears I faintly hear commands being given from the trenches behind mine, I can't discern what orders are being given but I know that no one will be coming to rescue me. I foolishly was one of four privates that volunteered to lead the advance on the German Mauser trench, I thought at the time that I could get the bastards, repay papa. How wrong was I, now three days later only I remain, the other three already going over the top heroically only to be cut down like animals, the first two only making it a few meters from our trench before being mowed down by the clack clack clack of the automatic weapon, an arm being cut clean away, a leg being ripped from another torso, their screams remain embedded in my mind, screaming in agony as the bullets kept on flying, kept on ripping through flesh until their voices were silenced. Only then once their bodies were still, holes ripped clean through, limbs torn off, cries for mercy, only then did the clack.. Clacking stop. Only then did the silence fill my mind, no sound, nothing, no birds no orders, no cries of agony nothing just empty space where there should be noise. It was the first time that I had seen killing up close, I never knew their names; it is like that here in these trenches of hell, no point in asking the men next to you their names as they may be dead by morning. But to see killing that close, to smell the blood, the cordite, to feel the air move close to your face as a bullet whizzes by, almost feels unreal.

    I didn't really know what to expect, who would. All I know is that that first time, that first moment when I saw those bodies jumping and jerking about as the 7.92 rounds ripped through their bodies, like they were dancing manikins that first spatter of blood I felt upon my face, even from ten feet away, shocked me, frightened me to my core, my mind froze and I wet myself. I had seen others do it many times before but never really understood how utterly afraid they had felt; now I do…

  We, the remaining private and I had waited a full day before agreeing that we should go over, do our duty. Take out the Mauser post and open the way for the troops at our rear to advance, to spill forward and kill every last one of those bastards who had taken my papa away from me. For hours we had waited planning our path, building our courage, praying to any gods that would listen for mercy, waiting for dusk, letting the sun lower its zenith behind us, in the hope it would give us a little cover as we breached the crest of our trench. Then finally our time was upon us, we could wait and stall no longer, we checked our rifles were clear and loaded, chappy, that's what he had said his name was earlier in the day, had said a short prayer and made the sign of the cross in front of us, then both counting to three chappy had charged over the top, he crested the trench and screaming his loudest war cry he had charged foreword stumbling through the thick goopy mud. I …. I had remained frozen to the ground.

  My legs refused to move, my mind screamed its order to move yet nothing happened, I was being held down by an invisible force, terror stricken I could not move. My heart pounded against my ribs as though trying to escape its bloody confinement, my lungs rapidly filled and emptied as I breathed in the damp feted trench air. All I was left to do was to watch, watch in slow motion, as though time had somehow been slowed down by half its speed. Watch, watch as chappy, now moving like a mime artist slowly moved his body forward, slowly pulling at one leg which had become stuck fast in the mud, pulling, pulling, and slowly, painfully slowly it freeing with a stretched drawn out plooooooop it came free, his war cry sounding like a single syllable being repeated over and over, his arms rotating over and over as he held his rifle high above his head trying to find an ounce of balance.

And then it began…. The claaaccckkk claaacckk claacckk of the Mauser. My voice freeing itself from its temporary proralisses I began to scream a soundless warning…. A warning which came far too late for even before the stretched out sounds burst from my mouth the first of the mausers rounds had found their target, stunned I watched the bullet flying towards chappys throat, I could see it spinning over and over, its surface shining, reflecting the last of the falling lights rays. Unable to stop its forward trajectory I could only watch dumbstruck as it impacted chappys throat dimpling the skin just below his jaw on the left hand side of his neck, slowly the dimple grew deeper and deeper until the skin was unable to stretch anymore, the bullet, still slowly spinning tore through the flesh turning its way deeper into his throat, I could even read the stamping on its bottom it was turning so slowly. Deeper still it ploughed burying itself. Only when the bullet was fully half way through did chappy begin to react, his face slowly began to twist and contort and the realization hit his mind like a steam train. His body began moving backwards, his feet still stuck fast in the mud. I felt that time was moving so slow that I could have ran over to chappy and lifted him out of harms ways, if only I could move, if only my body would let me help my friend. Chappys neck began to deform at the rear, the bullet forcing its way forward and out on its killing path, again the skin stretching to its fullest before erupting open, spewing forth the bullet and torn flesh, the wound fully as large as a man's hand. Flesh, skin, muscle, sinew and blood bursting free as though from a volcano...

   Just as suddenly as everything had slowed down it now sped back up to normal speed, clack... clack...clack.. The mauser screamed, spitting its hot lethal bullets in rapid fire into chappy, several more ravaging his throat before he began to fall, hopefully already dead as the hot spinning projectiles continued slamming into him, one taking out an eye, another exploding against teeth, his body jerking with each impact, the bullets dropping with his body until it hit the muddy ground, even then the bastards didn't stop, they kept on pummeling him with rounds using his prone body for target practice. For the second time in as many days I felt the warm wet sensation filling my underwear as I wet myself, this finally triggering my body into movement, I collapsed to the muddy ground tears streaming down my face and there I remained, curled up hold my rifle tightly against my chest, sobbing.

   That had been countless hours ago, a lifetime it felt like, I had remained there frozen in my fetal position, sobbing, want to be home again in the warm embrace of my mother. I longed to feel the sun on my face, to smell the clean air of home, to taste mothers hot potato pie smothered in thick gravy but I knew deep down that I never would hold my mother again, I would never see her or home again, I knew in my heart that I had to go over, to do my duty for my country, for my papa. This was my fate, to be gunned down in some rotten field far from home in a country that I'd never knew.

   I dug deep within myself for the courage to do what I had to, lifting my head from the sodden mud my mind screamed at my muscles to move, inch by inch my body lifted itself up, higher and higher I rose then forward I moved, all was silent around me, a whisper sounding like a thunderclap, my rifle was loaded and cocked, my heart beating its thunder drums against my chest, my jaw clenched tightly its muscles twitching, my legs finding a new strength, powering me forward, up up and over I raced, my sights firmly set on the mauser trench 50 yards in front of me. Like a raging animal bursting from the thick jungle I breached the top of the trench and ploughed onwards, now nothing would stop me my resolve firm, my mind steeled ready for the onslaught, kill or be killed there simply was no other choice, the mud trying its best to hold my boots captive, each step proceeded by a plop as it lost its gooey grip before once again regaining it.

   Forward I surged, fully two meters I had traversed and still no clack clack clack.. They must have seen me by now, heard my plopping progress towards them…I felt a glimmer of hope as I trudged onwards, maybe, just maybe I would surprise them, hope began to finger its way slowly into my mind, yes I would be upon them before they knew I was coming, I would have my revenge for papa for my fallen brothers, I would kill every last one of those bastards, I would look deep into each man's eyes as I ended his life, watch as the light in his eyes faded, he would see me, see me and know that it was me, a mere boy who had bested him, I who had sent him on his way to hell for what he had done, for the lives he had wiped out. They would all pay…

   Already in just a few seconds I had reached my fallen friends, there not a few feet from me they lay twisted and prone, their bodies already beginning to rot in this foul mud, body parts torn off, skin ripped away from flesh, eyes blown out and teeth smashed through. For you brothers, I'll get those bastards for you ill ki…….

   So wrapped up in my hatred, so fuelled by adrenaline was I that I didn't even feel the first round which tore through my shin taking flesh and bone with it as it exploded out the back of my leg, so deafened was I by the sound of rage that I never heard the voluminous clack… clack… clack.. Of their Mauser as it once again began its symphony of death, resonating its musical notes of destruction, plucking away at its strings of agony.

   Not until my leg was torn away from under myself did I finally awaken to the hell I was in, my left leg had been severed just below the knee, my bloody stump already plunging itself deeply into the mud, my rifle falling from my grasp as another 7.92 shell bit its way into my right hand, the impact blowing off three fingers and a thumb. Like snakes of iron the bullets bit me, a constant barrage , one after another, my body became no more than a bloody sieve , arms, legs chest throat and head, nothing was left untouched, yet even through all of the onslaught I felt no pain, no agony, nothing. It was as if my mind had left my body and I watched the ravage take place from afar.

   Pain had left me; it had given me the grace of pure emptiness, a void from feeling. Not even when the last shell tore through my throat ripping out my spine did I feel any more than the kiss of an angel.

   Unable to hold itself up my head fell, chin hitting my chest, I knew I was dying, I knew that Christ would be soon collecting another soul from this field of torment but all I could do was to look into the face of my fallen friend in front of me, my body toppling , unable to use any limb to save myself I fell, my face hitting the wet mud, my jaw braking with the impact, an eye ball popping as its thick fluid trickled onto my watery grave, and as I died, as my light upon this world slowly dimmed I looked into the face of the fallen private and saw myself, the face before me I knew so well, I had looked upon it a hundred times in our mirror back home, I looked upon myself laying prone, twisted, ravaged in that wet bloody mud filled field. It was me laying there dead. I had gone over the top with chappy, I had been cut down by the mauser spitting its rounds through me and chappy, but my mind had stayed behind, it had watched me being ripped apart by the white hot bullets, my soul had stayed, stayed to watch and wait. My mind had saved me, mother I'm coming home... darkness filled my vision in my remaining eye... Darkness wrapped its arms around me like a blanket of nothingness... Darkness whispered sweet sonnets of pleasure in my ears and closed away the world from my mind; just a fallen private in a muddy grave closes his eyes and sleeps......

THE END

Hell burp

Cage placed his knife and fork back down onto the table in front of himself, the meal had been everything that he had hoped, it should have been at the prices printed on the menu's which the overly friendly waiter had produced. The stake had been brazed to perfection, its accompanying sources had spun his palette into a cacophony of taste, each mouthful had given his senses a new enlightenment of wonder matched only by the delicate bouquet of the vintage '47 wine. Hell his publisher was picking up the tab for this one so why shouldn't he indulge a little, to hell with his waist line. Looking across the table he could see that the meal had given Ruby his publishing agent as much pleasure as himself, her eyes were slightly glazed, her lips full with the blood rushing through them and her cheeks held a slight blush, hell she looked as though an unseen gigolo had been slowly building her arousal from under the table, bringing her close to rapture but just holding off from the final tantalising lap of his or her tongue.

   Realising his gaze had drifted down to rest on her more than ample breasts Cage slapped his full stomach and looked up into Ruby's deep green eyes. He found her rather attractive, if a little on the thin side for his taste but still more than once he had pleasured himself whilst holding an image of her naked writhing body beneath his, her long dark hair being thrown forward as she screams his name, gouging deep scratches down his back as her orgasm tightens her vulva sending him over the edge, two bodies melding as one twisting and contorting in the heat of ecstasy.

'So cage, you told me on the phone that you have finished the second draft.' Ruby's voice shattering the image and stamping him back into this reality.

Rapidly gathering his thoughts Cage lifted his silk napkin to his mouth in an attempt to hide his slight blush. Nodding in agreement he opened his mouth to reply when before he knew it was happening a loud long belch escaped, not just a small insignificant burp, no this one came from his toes, it built in strength and volume as it thundered up through his chest, Cage's throat vibrated as the burp erupted. Other diners seated around failed to disguise their shock at the sudden voluminous outburst, some even dropping their cutlery in their surprise.

'Oh my, please Ruby do excuse me, I must say I think that one came from the pit of hell.' Cage dropped his napkin and lowered his gaze in the hope of avoiding eye contact with any of the startled diners.

Now dear readers this is where I feel I must interrupt for a moment if I may. You see even though most of the highly influential and well to be diners most certainly did hear Cage's bodily outburst what every one of those hip diners, including Ruby, why including Cage himself, what everyone in the restaurant failed to see, could not now or ever see was in fact the birth of a creature born not of this world. I shall try my best to explain exactly what happened the moment that Cage burped and the following moments directly after, but please keep in mind the fact that no one there ever knew of the following events.

Reset. Ok

Rapidly gathering his thoughts cage lifted his silk napkin to his mouth in an attempt to hide his slight blush. Nodding in agreement he opened his mouth to reply when before he knew it was happening a loud long belch escaped, not just a small insignificant burp, no this one came from his toes, it built in strength and volume as it thundered up through his chest, Cages throat vibrated as the burp erupted. Even before the whole sound had left Cage's throat time slowed to a thousandth of its normal rate, the seated diners in the restaurant moved but it was as though each one had become a stop animation puppet, their motions were so slow it was like looking at a film each cell at a time. Each of the vibrations rippled through Cage's throat like waves through jelly only slowed to less than a heart beat of the universe, its momentum causing tiny ripples to walk across the skin, each taking a lifetime to cross the desert of follicles. Beginning at the edge of time Cage's mouth began to stretch wider and wider, at each corner of his mouth small black talons hooked themselves over its edge from inside, then two more, then two more still. With painfully slow speed theses pure black talons continued their forward outward journey, one, then two, then finally three raw flesh knuckles freed themselves next, something, something foul, something not of this earth was slowly clawing its way out of cage's mouth. As time had all but stopped no reaction could be given by cage himself or those directly around him, all of this was happening outside to constraints of time as we know it. The three fingered hands, if its possible to call them that slowly stretched cage's mouth wider and wider, impossibly wide, his skin should have split in a fountain of blood, his jaw should have been ripped free from his skull and cast upon the table as a discarded relic of humanity, but please remember all of these travesties were happening beyond our comprehension of time. Two long slender and totally skinless arms thrust their way out into the awaiting world, their elbows twisting in the wrong direction and there at the outward bend of each a large glistening black claw, the arms twisted and writhed as the thing, the abortion from hell fought with this pain of existence to free itself from the wet embrace of cage's mouth.

   With a scream which only a mother nurturing her dead rotting baby can release the thing thrust its head, sorry thrust what I think was its head up and out spawning its feted breath into our world. The head was neither round nor was it oval, it more resembled the twisted rotting remains of some unborn and uncreated foetus, the top of the head almost flat and open, its interior swam with a foul smelling obsidian blackness. Even now I wake from the nightmares that I have seen held within that succubus's cranium. Eyeless, no mouth or nose, skinless and devoid of form it still somehow emanated the blood curdling scream, never stopping to take a breath, just continuous pain and suffering, if ever that could be put into a sound then that is what this thing was spewing forth. Using its elbow claws for leverage it dragged the rest of its bloody rotting body out of cage's mouth landing upon the table with an audible plop. It painfully lifted itself up onto the two short stumps, again devoid of skin only showing raw rotting flesh and slime, planting its two three toed hoofs wide it arched backwards and bent double as though it had no spine. The whole demonic thing standing no more the two feet tall.

   Using its talons it clicked rhythmically on the table before its form quivered as though caught in a brisk chill. Using unseen power it leapt in one bound from the table landing almost at the restaurants door, pausing only briefly to survey its surroundings the thing then simply walked through the thick heavy plated glass door and out onto the street, swaying gently it again bent double but this time forward as though touching its hellish toes and leapt clear across the street landing directly in front of an old little lady who happened to be in mid sneeze, mouth open head slightly back, hand about to reach up to cover her face.

   Without warning and as fast as the thing had birthed itself from cage's mouth it now entered the old ladies, throwing itself towards her face then stretching out flat at the last moment, wasting no time it writhed and contorted its hell spawned body, twisting and writhing it rapidily clawed its way down inside the unsuspecting old ladys mouth, with a flick of its middle talon it disappeared and was gone. As though someone had flicked a switch all time resumed its endless tick, everything, everyone resumed their place back in the universe.

   As cage made his apologises for the sudden belch, outside the restaurant across the street an old lady sneezed into their hand, stopped raised her head and snapped it to her left, her eyes had taken to obsidian black. Turning she altered her course.

   The taxi never had a chance, the old lady had come from nowhere, it's driver had hit the brakes but only after the old lady had buried her face into its windscreen, the impact snapping her neck instantly. By the time the taxi had finally come to a halt full two thirds of her body had been swallowed by the cab, an arm being ripped free and an eye being popped. As the last of her soul raised from her smashed body a small impish demon was returning to hell its work done... for now..

THE END

FREAK SHOW

" Roll up roll up come and see the fascinating wonders of the world, yes for the small price of the admission fee you can gaze upon the wonders brought to you from the far dark corners of the world. Sights the like of which you have never seen before, sights that will awe you, sights that will scare you, sights that will make your blood run cold. Come one come all the show is about to begin so quickly now purchase your ticket and join the line as we are about to explore the world of wonder."

The loud speakers cackled as the announcer replaced the microphone back onto its stand. Looking out at the milling crowd below him he rubbed his itching side and thought to himself, good crowd in, should make a pretty penny with this afternoons show, that is if those freaks behave themselves this time, not like last week when two of them, Gill and Phill, the main attraction up and went for the spectators, broke the bloody glass on their tank and tried to paw some paying customers. Well I soon put a stop to that, he thought grinning to himself, and they won't be smashing anything in a good while. Still smiling to himself he disappeared behind the heavy painted canvas to prepare for the show.

  Slowly the waiting crowd shuffled forward one pace then stopped. Like a string of hanging lights they stretched out along the edge of the carnival tenting. Each one waiting expectantly to enter the brightly painted canvassed opening, waiting to gaze upon the freaks and disturbing sights which waited for them inside, each clutching tightly their entrance ticket as though it were a trophy. Every few moments shuffling forwards, slowly drawing nearer and nearer to their prize, but for Zion they moved too slowly, impatiently he swayed from side to side, this would be his first time to gaze upon the wonders inside, his parents not allowing him to do so until now, not until his father had spoken up on the journey here, saying that he thought the time had come for Zion to see for himself the sights of which he had only read about and heard of from his older friends, finally he would get to gaze at the freaks and see how deformed and disfigured they really were. He steeled himself that he would not look away or shy from them, not like his brother had done last year when the carnival had come to their small town, just as it did each year, each summer it would visit his small town for one week and one week only, then at the completion of the seventh day the whole carnival would pack up and leave, well leave isn't really the right word, it would simply vanish, it would suddenly be there, appear on the same patch of ground each year, unannounced it would arrive. Then just as quickly it would disappear once the week was over, no one would ever see it appear or vanish, even those who had stayed behind on purpose to watch it go would always seem to fall asleep or happen to be looking away when pop it would vanish.

"Settle down Zion, it won't be long till we are inside now" Zion's dad said in a gravelly voice.

I can't. Thought Zion. Are you kidding me dad? I'm about to see them, the things I've read about so much, I'm actually going to see them monsters, I'm going to wet myself if we don't hurry up I'm so excited he thought.

Again the crowd shuffled forward, but this time instead of stopping after one pace they continued moving, granted at a snail's pace but forward they moved, each plodding on closer and closer to the entrance with its bright gaudy paintings of monsters and freaks. Zion looked up at them and wondered if they were paintings of the freaks inside he was about to see, he hoped not as some of the monsters on the huge canvasses didn't look all that scary, some of the paintings he thought looked quite badly done,

I bet I could paint that one better he mused. I'm going to paint them, I'm going to paint all the monsters and freaks that I see when I get back home, I'm going to paint them all and I bet they will be better than these ones. He thought.

   Looking around he saw that the line was disappearing into the opening which had a large painted sign above. It read

   'Entrance' Beware the beasts and monsters don't get you.

   Yeh ok he thought.

 As though just to remind him his stomach did another quick flip, a little bile playing in his mouth. He wasn't scared, well not really, maybe a little, he knew his dad was here by his side, he wouldn't let anything happen to him but still he was a little bit nervous, just a little bit mind you. Butterflies had been playing rugby in his stomach all morning ever since his dad had said today was the day he could see the wonders for himself.

I bet all my friends, the ones that had already seen the monsters felt the same before they went in, he thought. Why even my brother had cried and been a girly girly legs all squarly after he had gone in, dad had had to take him straight home after, mom had shouted at dad saying he was too young to see things like that and what had he been thinking taking him in there, my dad had simply chuckled and walked away shaking his head.

No. Zion thought, im not going to cry or be a grily squirly, im going to be tough and look those monsters right in the face and not look away, not even if they growl or hit the cages at me, I think, well im sure I wont cry, wont I. he thought.

   Holycrap even before he realized it it was their turn, they had reached the ticket booth whilst he had been deep in thought,

"This is it, this is it". He kept telling himself.

   "Two tickets to the show please." Zion's dad spoke into the little round voice -plate cut into the glass window of the booth as he dropping several coins onto the counter top.

   The ticket seller leaned closer to the pane and fixed Zion with a stare which made him feel uncomfortable.

   "He's a little small don't you think?" the seller asked

   "Why not at all, he's just the right size to see his first show, don't you think ?" dad said dropping a few more coins onto the counter.

The ticket seller sniffed, lifted his gaze lazily to dad and scooped the coins off the counter replacing them with two bright red tickets,

"Just keep him close, don't want no young one's being lost in our show. Now move along." He said

Dad took the two tickets nodded his head and ushered Zion forward along the side of the ticket booth and on through the heavy canvass and into the start of the show.

"What did he mean dad lost young one's in the show?" asked Zion.

His dad looked down, "Don't pay any attention to him son, these carnie folk are a bit strange."
Zion followed his dad into the dim interior of the show, several others had gathered around what looked like a doorway on the opposite end of a narrow canvassed corridor. Only one light was fixed to a pole behind Zion and his dad so the corridor was wrapped mostly in shadows, the side canverses looked old and grimy, they looked to Zion as though they had never been cleaned some of them had brown stains over them. Zion could feel the fear slowly clawing its way up from his belly, as the two moved forward he moved just a little closer to dad.

Those in front had already passed through the small doorway in front of Zion so now it was his turn, his and his dads. Bracing himself he followed dad through.

The next room seemed huge to Zion, far larger than the outside looked. It was brightly lit, almost too bright; Zion found that he had to squint a little in order to close out some of the penetrating light. He looked around in awe trying to take in all the sights in one go, around the outer edges of the room stood tall glass cases, probably twenty in total, each one Zion guessed was about 8 units high, 5 units wide and just as many units deep. It looked like there was a single freak in some of the cases, other cases held two, sometimes three of four freaks. Then there in the center of the room Zion saw a huge case fully four times as large as the others, glass side's all round and inside, well inside Zion counted at least ten of the freaks, most slowly moving around gazing out at the spectators gazing in.

"Well, go on then Zion. Go take a look but remember don't get too close to the glass." Said dad

Zion moved forward towards the center of the room, towards the largest of the cases, the fear tightening its grip, his stomach threatening to eject itself at any moment. Slowly he drew closer and closer until he was almost touching the glass in front of him, stunned he gazed in awe at the hideous sights inside, his mind fighting to accept the horrors which he gazed upon.

The freak in the case closest to Zion lifted his head and walked over to the glass, the rough ground bit into his naked feet, the collar cutting into the soft flesh of his neck. Zion forced himself to take in every detail of the freak that now stood in front of him.

The thing, the freak stood almost as tall as dad, it seemed to be holding itself up with two growths coming from its middle form, these two stick like things were bending in the middle, they went up to a kind of trunk like center, some of it was covered in a fine straw like matting, the middle part had another two longish growths poking out, one each side. On the end of these growth like protrusions Zion saw what looked like five sticks, but the thing, the freak was able to move these sticks. Zion was having trouble believing what he was seeing, his mind doubting the reality of what was in the case before him. Looking higher Zion saw a blob sticking out from the top of the center; it had two orbs that were moving about and an opening in it that kept closing, muffled sounds were coming from this hole. He had heard these things, these freaks called humans but he never thought he would here in a room full of them.

Its horrible thought Zion

"I know son it's hard to believe that things as hideous as these can exist, but now you can see that freaks are real, they do exist but thankfully only here in the show." Spoke dad

Its mass quivered with the forward motion, like some kind of bloody festering mass of slime it came closer, almost touching the glass, it moved like a snail or slug, its form slithering forward across the rough ground, it had no real form, its surface seemed to undulate and writhe, it glistened and shimmered as though wet, a rainbow of colors flashed across its surface, there seemed no beginning or end to its structure, just one rolling, pulsing mass.

Leon's mind screamed, looking out from inside the clear cage he struck the glass again and again in frustration and fear. the thing outside came closer, its form rippeling, Leons mind swam.
" what the fuck is going on, how did I get here" he screamed….

THE END

SUICIDE

Two lone figures are sat a little distance apart, their legs dangle over the edge of a deep abyss, they are both deep in conversation with each other, both oblivious to the silent night around themselves, the air lays still and heavy like a blanket covering the world.

Figure one looks out over the endless darkness, surveying its vast expanse of emptiness his eyes fight hard to pick out a single shadow. Slowly turning his head towards the second seated figure he speaks. "I would have done it differently, all of it I mean, I don't think there's a thing that I wouldn't have changed." his voice low and gravely, course like sandpaper.

From his left, figure two spins his head round to face him, throwing his main of long blond hair back across his shoulders as he does so. "well unfortunately that's the kick, we can only ever see the error of our lives when its at an end, right or wrong I guess it has to be that way, otherwise we would unbalance the scales." he replies.

Figure one lifts his right hand up almost to shoulder height, with his pam turned skyward he focuses his attention on its centre. A few centimetres above his palm the air itself begins to twist, slowly at first no more than a breath but then building, turning round and round like its caught in a mixer, gradually a small twister, no larger than a fist forms above his open palm; as it spins ever faster and faster it begins to glow, white at first then yellow red and orange, the spinning rainbow of a twister suddenly bursts into a tower of flames, round and round the flames fly, their heat burning, their light blinding. Figure one grins a malnevolant evil grin as a thousand babies cry out at once, a black glistening forked tongue, snake like, slithers its way out and wets his drawn lips with fresh blood.

Figure two shakes his head as he watches the display of vanity. "Ive told you before, if you keep playing with it you'll go blind."

With a rapid clench of his fist the flames are extinguished in a puff of dark acrid smoke, "spoilsport." he says turning back to look at figure two, the evil rancid grin still fitted to his face. "that's your kinds problem, never know how to enjoy yourselves, always doing the right thing, always trying to please you know who, always thinking of the consequences."

Lifting his own left hand figure two continues to look over at his companion, from just above his palm a small spark of light appears, "oh we have fun to." as he speaks the light grows in intensity, its brightness grows with each passing second, brighter and brighter it grows, it becomes the centre of atomic fusion then on passed, not even stopping as it reaches the suns strength. Its his time to grin.

From his right comes a whimper of ten thousand souls, "enough. Stop it, it burns" figure one cries out. He holds up his arms to shield from the light, the raw skin blisters and boils, his face contorts as it begins to melt.

A small child like giggle escapes the lips of figure two, "you see we can have fun also" he said clapping together his hands, the light blinked back out of existence. Lifting his head towards the darkened sky he closes his eyes takes a deep breath then continues. "lets get on with this, we will never agree or even agree to disagree with each other, we are to perform our duties so lets just put aside the things we have no control over. Now by my recognin you took the last so this times is mine."

Figure one spat forth a verse of language never spoken on earth, never spoken on any planet. He spat the sounds and followed them with a globule of blood, the plasma filled flehm flew far into the nothingness before being swallowed up by it. "fine." he spat " but as I recall it the last choose neither you nor me, so as I see it that was a draw, your getting old, old man."

Holding up his hand in resignation figure two nodded his head. "ok, ok I forgot about that one, I'm sure you can find a little forgiveness in you somewhere, it has been an age as you know. Our purpose takes its toll as does the ages; but as I recall our last only chose not to chose because you offered the void, making it a void outcome, so as was written before time I put to you that we settle this by the old way. Are you ready ?" he asked "agreed, begin"

"one. Two. Three."

As the words were spoken both figures held aloft their hands, with each count they thundered a clenched fist onto an open palm, the skies erupted with lightening at each impact, the winds blew hard and the ground shook. At the third count figure two's clenched fist opened as he held two fingers forward. At the same instant figure one smashed his fist onto his outreached palm and held it there.

"ahh you see" he boomed " rock blunts scissors, you loose this ones mine."

Figure two hung his head down, resting his chin upon his chest, as the winds blew he slowly began to disappear, like vapour his very being dematerialized in an ethereal smoke until completely gone; at the same time as his bodies disillusion the skies lightened, a figure slowly formed beneath figure one, a huge human form slowly took solidity into the light. Figure one stood, took a few steps froward and leaned inward, resting his hands against the giants earlobe he softly whispered into the cavernous ear before to disappearing.

Pushing the muzzle firmly into her mouth she closed her eyes tightly and reached down for the Trigger, " that's right what have I got to live for" she thought pulling at its steely coldness.

The exploding shell tore through her mouth, tearing aside flesh and muscle as it spun its way up, up through her screaming brain and out into the thunderous night, the top of her head erupted in an explosion of brain and bone, the shotgun fell to the floor clattering as her head fell forward. Slowly a long lazy spittle of blood, brain and fluid dripped to the floor. Another life lost, another soul won, the war continues the fight just begun.........

THE END

THE BAND

'It's your acceptance, of the annihilation of the human fucking race that means it has begun. You twist your mind and open your eyes to the horror's as you watch the fun. Don't stop the hate, the killing has only just began. We serve your souls and drink the blood, our rage never stops until we are done.'

The masked singer spat the words into his wireless mic, in turn the 60 amps which filled the arena machine gunned them out into raging crowd as though they were bullets. Standing atop the centre monitor he looked out over the 50,000 strong crowd, he held each and every one in the palm of his hand, for the last 90 minutes they had screamed, shouted moshed, danced and raised hell whilst the band had given them a show to stop all shows. The crowd was caressed moulded and stroked into frenzy by the relentless music, each note thundering out through the arena, the bass and drums so resonate that it impacted the fans chests like a punch.

As though sensing the finally was close the crowd surged as one, like a mass of worker ants they pushed forward, each trying their best to gain enough space to advance forward, elbows were freely swung out, kicks randomly sent, anything that would get them closer to the stage, closer to their gods. Bodies were pushed and shoved, some fell and disappeared underneath the feet of the advancing ants, some were lifted and held high. Bruce was one of those being lifted, higher and higher. He knew it was pointless to fight for his freedom, he simply had to ride the sea of clutching hands, he became a thrash surfer riding the rising and falling waves of hands, some clutched, others gripped, some even groped, for those ones Bruce hit out with his fists. Bobbing up and down he moved, forward, onward closer and closer towards the stage he rode the waves. Then as quickly as he had begun his wave time it ended, being discarded over the front barrier like a unwanted memory he was tossed landing on the hard concrete floor. Jumping to his feet Bruce quickly searched left and right, he knew from experience that he didn't have long before security would take hold of him and roughly toss him back into the crowd, or worse throw him out of the gig.

Bruce's luck was with him, off to his left one of the security guards had already taken hold of another helpless surfer and was making his way away to the stages left exit. Bruce looked right and grinned. A monster of a security guard, muscles all bulging, veins all popping was just at that second being used as a landing mat for a female surfer, both guard and surfer folding into one mass as they both hit the floor. Bruce knew this was his one opportunity and didn't waste it, turning round to the stage the leapt across the ten foot no man's land. The stage stood shoulder height but using a speed and power born of rage using his hands as levers he leapt clean up onto the stage. There not four feet away from him, still standing on top of the centre monitor was Rage the front man and lead singer. Holding both hands above his head Bruce began to cross the four foot gap, he made devil horns with both hands.

It came from out of nowhere, the monster of a security guard speared Bruce from his right. The sudden unexpected impact folding Bruce in half, the breath burst from his lungs, a sound between a grunt and a cough along with a little spittle escaped his mouth. His body was airborne for what to Bruce felt like weeks, he watched the bright stage lights moving away at a snail's pace, even now his mind not quite catching up, then his senses burst to life as he felt himself and the guard falling, falling down.

'Shit his mind yelled at him, the guard must have taken us both clean off the stage.'

In answer he felt his body begin its impact with the hard concrete, he began but never finished feeling the full impact of the landing because he simply passed out, the guards impact and the sudden jolt to his head rendered him unconscious, which I guess was a good thing. Like a professional wrestler the security guard rolled to the right on impact, taking most of the force with his massive bulging shoulder. Gaining his feet like a panther he grabbed the prone body of Bruce threw it over his shoulder, turning his gaze to the stage he made eye contact with Rage who simply gave a small nod of his head. Message understood the guard calmly walked out and round to the back stage area.

Rage surveyed his fans and the ensuing carnage, lifting his head he spat watching its arc through the air, lifting the mic he growled to the crowd

'Cardiff, make some fucking noise for me'

The crowd drunk on chaos screamed for all they were worth.

The band played their frenzied instrumental its tempo rising and rising washing away the crowd's sins, pointing at them Rage spoke

'As always my children you have torn the fucking roof off this place tonight. Now we will see you all here again very soon my legion, so for now from all of us here it's good night until the next.' Rage raised his mic arm high above his head as the music reached a fevered pitch, he gazed out over the jumping crowd then dropped his hand, instantly the music stopped and the whole stage light up with pyros, their heat singing the back of the securities heads, the light blinding the screaming crowd and the shock wave hitting their chests and physically pushing them back. Lights went out, the stage fell into darkness and the show was over.

THE END

SHOPPING LIST

With Her cheeks, still wet from the tears Stacey brought the car to a jerky stop. Wiping away the damp sorrow trails with the back of her hand she breathed deeply and looked at her reflection in the rear-view mirror; she hardly knew the girl staring back at her anymore, the past four years had taken their toll on both her looks and her mental health. It had all started so great, the relationship had begun in a whirlwind of fun, expectation and sex, the sex had been nothing like she had experienced before, wild furious and spontaneous. Unfortunately like most things in her relationship with Drake the sex had changed, the fun had changed, the spontaneity had changed, gradually the arguments had begun, slowly, simply, small disagreements at first, but then they became more and more heated, more frequent, more hate based; and then the violence had begun, by then she felt as though there was no way out, like she was to blame; a little misplaced item or a flippant retort would be used as kindle in the fire by Drake, he would follow mostly the same pattern, the silence, then the raised voice followed by the torrent of foul names and then the abuse, most times it would only be a hard slap or a back hand, sometimes if Stacey had pushed things too hard then he would use a closed fist, always to the body or legs as not to leave any visible marks and never to the face, somehow he always found the restraint to not hit her face, at least he loved her enough not to mark her face. Like most abused partners Stacey believed that the punishment was her doing, she was at fault and to blame, as always Drake would leave to return the next day with a gift, chocolates or flowers, and as always the promises would follow, promises of how he never meant to hurt her, how he would never do this again, and always the twist of, if only she would take a little more care in her looks or wore the clothes that he thought she should be wearing, the accusations of flirting with other men whilst he was at work all day; he had even taken away her mobile phone, insisting on being present whenever she would call her widowed mum. Slowly through the years her friends had fallen away, some trying to make her see that things weren't right, but Drake had stopped these from having any contact with her.

Stacey fought back a new wave of tears and stared deeply into her own eyes reflected back. 'I hate him' she thought. Holding the mirror with both shaking hands she steeled herself then through clenched teeth she shouted "I wish Drake was dead. This is the last time; he's is never going to lay a hand on me again; I'm done." In her mind the decision had been made, she would go, leave him, pack some clothes and just go, go anywhere that was away from Drake, she should have done this years ago. 'why have I waited this long?' she thought. 'no, he can go to hell'.

"right ill pick up a few things, some toiletries and some snacks for the trip." Stacey said to no one in general as she strode in through the supermarkets sliding glass doors, her stride was confident, her step had purpose, she felt a change in herself; yes, her ribs hurt from the punches and it hurt a little to take a breath but with her new resolve came a determination, a feeling of strength that she once had in herself but somehow had lost, she felt she had found it once again, she felt like she could do this, like nothing could stop her. As she took a shopping basket and made her way down the first aisle, she even gave a little smile to a male store worker restocking a shelf with top brand cookies.

   With her new found confidence Stacey danced her way round the stacked shelves, picking out items that she hadn't been allowed to buy for the last few years, a soft delicate deodorant, a new glitter scrunchy, some sugar laced treats and even a bottle of her once favourite schnapps. Half way down the next isle Stacey glanced over and spotted the hair dye section, she thought for a moment then walked over and picked up a box of blossom red, it promised to change your hair colour to a vibrant blossom red, but what caught her attention more was the slogan printed on the box, 'Dare to change the women that you are' it promised.

   "yes, I dare" she said out loud and gave a small giggle as she tossed the box into her basket before moving further down the aisle. Above and to her left she spotted a clear glass jar of face cream, raising up on to tiptoe Stacey reached up and took hold of a jar, at the same moment a stabbing pain from one of her cracked ribs made her winch causing her grip to loosen, the jar slipped from her grasp and silently tumbled through the air, like a movie played in slow motion she watched unable to move as the jar sailed towards the ground, over and over it tumbled, the stores bright lights caught the polished glass turning it into a mini disco ball. Down and down, it fell until its path became obstructed by the floor; with an almighty thunderous clash the glass jar exploded spewing its contents across the store floor, shards of broken glass scattered in all directions; the shuddering impact breaking the motion spell, everything instantly began to play at normal speed. Stacey jumped at the sound of the impact dropping her basket she grasped herself in a shocked hug.

As though from nowhere a store college rounded the corner and rushed over to Stacey. "miss, miss are you ok?" she asked.

The words broke the spell, Stacey looked from the store college to the floor then back, "oh dear, I'm really sorry, I've dropped. Here let me clean this mess." Stacey said as she dropped to her knees and began gathering up pieces of the broken jar.

"miss, that's not nesicery. Please I'll just go and get someone from clean up" the college said leaving Stacey on her knees.

Stacey frantically grasped the broken fragments of glass, not even noticing as some began to slice into her hand, all she knew was she had to clean the mess up before Drake saw it, he would be furious. Spinning round and reaching down to retrieve a large piece Stacey noticed that the reflection in the glass looked like a tiny tv screen with moving figures, as she looked closer more and more of the fragments seemed to be all playing the same scene, slowly magically the fragments seemed to grow, they started to melt and to flow like gel, each finding its partner before forming one larger piece, two became one, and so it went; in a matter of seconds the fragments had become one large looking glass about two feet in diameter, Stacey stared mesmerised by the liquid curiosity happening right Infront of her. The large fragment held its round shape but for only a second before it began to twist and miss form, the reflection had become one of fire or rather of flames, the floor beneath the changing shape began to fall away as though the ground beneath it were collapsing, bit by bit the floor disintergrated, a tower of flames two feet high jumped up from the open chasm; the edges of the opening had seemed to have solidified as Stacey now found herself looking down into a fiery deep abyss, she could feel the heat given by the flames, she could taste the acrid smoke, her eyes saw it but her mind screamed in denial. She risked a glance around herself but found that she was alone, an attempt to stand told her that she had become frozen to the spot, so she did the only thing left to her and looked once again down into the flaming hole.

   The heat emitting from the flaming void burnt her face, Stacey's lips felt taught and slightly cracked. A liquid vision slowly swam into focus nestled between the flames; the void now a full fifty feet deep was filled with craggy rocks, flames licking at their edges and there in the centre of this hell spawned vision stood two figures. Stacey leaned in closer to the void to see better, over balanced and found herself tumbling into it and down, down she fell tumbling over and over, the heat intense, her vision blurring before suddenly blinking out.

   Stacey came to with a few rapid blinks of her eyes, she found herself standing deep inside the void, the rock which she now found herself standing on was surrounded by flames, she felt the heat all around her, the air fiery with each breath. There in front of her, not four feet away stood Drake, or rather someone who looked like her Drake, how can this be she thought, the lookalike was stripped naked and somehow stood in an awkward pose, lifted onto tiptoes with both arms tightly held at his sides, his chest thrust forward shoulders back and his head held high, he looked straight up through the opening which Stacey had just fell; but what frightened her more was the way in which his body seemed to judder almost like an old video recorder set to pause, his torso would give a slight shiver and blur out of focus. If this horrific vision was not enough to shatter her mind then the thing which stood next to Drake would have sent anyone else's mind into shutdown.

   Stacey's mouth hung open a little as she tried to comprehend the sight before her. The thing in front of her stood around five feet tall, its form seemed to be made up of a constantly shifting mass, it had no discernible legs, instead where there should have been hips and legs the thing only had a rippling mass of raw skinless flesh, the flesh would twist and rotate, stretching and twisting over itself, this skinless flesh continued up the things torso stopping at a long snake like neck, this twisted back and forwards rippling with a rasping sound; at the end of this snake like limb was a pulsating opening, its edges wet and glistened as they rounded in back to the opening, it almost looked like some kind of giant earth worm, its open head filled with several rows of razor sharp triangular teeth, all moving back and forth clicking and clacking against one and another, the head always snaking, always weaving. Clear bile constantly dripped from this opening and as it fell to the rocks surface it sizzled and slowly burnt its way into the rock.

   Stacey jumped in shock as Drake screamed as unseen talons slowly tore a strip of skin two inches wide from his chest up to his shoulder, ripping off a nipple in the process, the flesh below glistened and convulsed. Strip after strip was torn from his upper torso by the unseen talons. With each new tear Drake would howl in anguish, his body remained fixed and his head tipped back but still the constant twitching remained, blood freely flowed down his body pooling around his bare feet, its thick red trails glistened and shone as the surrounding flames danced all round. This continued until the last scrap of skin remained on Drakes upper body, it resembled a skinned shank of meat hung ready for slicing, the screams of pain and agony had ceased, instead Drake could only sob. The skinless creature Infront of Stacey now turned its snake like protuberance towards her, its rows of sharp teeth quickening in their chattering.

A tortured voice filled Stacey's mind, low and strained it slowly spoke to her. "This is your wish. Is it not?" it asked. Then spoken as a statement of finality the voice said "here he will remain, remain for an eternity and learn to enjoy his suffering like no other can."

The realisation hit Stacey with the force of an actual blow, this was Drake, this was hell, she had wished for this, she had made this happen, this was her doing but, not what she wanted, her poor Drake being flailed like this for ever, no shaking her head she found her voice amongst the sobs and crackle of the flames.

"no, please no, I don't want this. Drake I'm sorry, please I didn't mean what I said, oh my god please no stop this." her voice crackling and fading as her tears found an exit. Throwing out her arms towards Drake Stacey screamed closing her eyes to shut out the horror she was witnessing; instantly the moment her eyelids closed the intense heat vanished, the flames receded back into the bowels of the void, Drakes sobbing ceased and the creature dissolved falling to the floor as a thick gel like substance, the void closed itself and the shards of glass once again scattered across the floor. Dropping her hands to her sides and opening her eyes Stacey found herself once again kneeling on the stores floor, the broken glass jar lay around her, its contents spread across the floor in all directions; there directly in front of her stood the store college mop and bucket in hand with a look of puzzlement on his face.

"I'm sorry, look at the mess. I have to go; I must get home to my Drake. Please I have to go." Stacey rose to her feet and turned to leave when the store college reached out and touched her arm, looking deeply into her eyes he spoke.

"be careful what you wish for." he said before he too slowly dissolved into thin air......

THE END

37

37 victims.

37 innocent lives brutally cut short.

37 innocent men and women savagely murdered, their bodies mutilated before each one being defiled in the most cruel and sickest way imaginable.

37 hopes and dreams callously cut short, and all by one man.

You Christen Garver are responsible for this fifteen-year killing spree, you Christen Garver sit here today bound, chained, shackled and in cuffs. Your home for the past twelve years being here, Holden state penitentiary, the last remaining penitentiary left in the whole of the United States of America which still carries out the order of the Death penalty. Lethal injection is to be your exit from this lonely solitary existence, a life of no remorse, one of no apathy or flickers of regret for these heinous crimes which you perpetrated.

"I have come in your final hours to offer you the lord's forgiveness, to share in his love for you. Through me you can ask for his forgiveness, he and only he alone can grant you access into the kingdom of heaven, it is through him and only through him our lord Jesus Christ can your soul be saved from an eternity of pain and suffering. I ask you my son, will you not ask for his forgiveness, will you not repent of your sins so that you may enter his kingdom of heaven, so that your everlasting soul may bathe in his light and his love." father Daimen spoke softly, a slight tremor to his voice.

Leaning heavily on the heavy metal table he looked directly into Christen's obsidian black eyes. "Chris, may I call you Chris.? I am giving you the chance to redeem your soul here now before it is too late, wont, won't you simply ask for the lord's forgiveness."

Chris sat motionless, unflinching. His deep black eyes locked with those of father Daimen. His chest rose and fell rhythmically. Overhead the single florescent light flickered out momentarily before spitting back into brightness, its soft yellowing glow adding nothing to the somber grey walled room. The air was thick with the smell of disinfectant and stale body Oder. Several days growth of stubble littered his face, dark shadows ringed his eyes adding to the blackness of its orbs, shoulder length unkempt dark hair finished of his hobo look.

"I ask forgiveness from no one, no man, no woman, no god. What I did, the things I have done I done out of want and lust. It is true I freed those 37 maggots of their weak and pointless lives. Each of those worthless pieces of meat begged me for death, each one I set free, me and no one else could lift them above this stench, this cesspit of depravity which you call life. I alone took them and gave them the gift of nothingness, the freedom of emptiness. No sorrow, no joy or hate or fear, no, now they can see the truth of it all." As Chris spoke, he slowly leaned in, lowering his shoulder's slightly, his stare intensifying.

Father Daimen sat back in his fixed chair, his grip tightening on the tattered copy of his bible. "Ok Chris, ok let's calm things a little, all I ask is that you share your soul with the lord to save yourself. Now is your time to seek redemption for your transgressions, the lord will forgive, all you need is to ask". Father Daimen took a small white handkerchief from his top pocket and slowly dabbed at the small beads of sweat which had formed there upon his forehead before continuing. "Will you not ask my son, relieve your soul of its burden and rejoice in the lord's forgiveness. Do not let your soul be damned for eternity, it is the lords will that we all walk amongst his light in heaven. Together we can seek his forgiveness. What do you think Chris?"

Chris's face remained as stone; no emotion crossed its craggy surface.

"Forgiveness. You pathetic fool, you say I should ask for your god's forgiveness. Your gods. Not mine. I have no belief in your god. He means no more to me than these worthless things that I set free, you see priest it's you that has things wrong, I'm not the one who is to be judged, no I'm not the one who can or will be judged, I... I am the one who judges, it's by my hands, by my mercy that I release these fools from their lives of false gods and their false servitude to a fractured world, one which praises the strong and scatters the weak. This travesty of a world which begs its worms to bow to its will, a world where the souls are scoured free of their own identity, of their own strength and honor. You talk to me of your god, he who suckles on the tit of humanity growing fat upon its foul milk of sorrow and weakness, your god that asks for these, these fucking animals to bow down in awe, to sacrifice their strengths as true beings of power. He Stifels their capacity to fulfil their true potential and stunts their abilities to become their true self's."

Spittle flew from Chris's mouth striking Father Daimen's face. The rage growing deep from within, his neck swelling as he strained against his restraints, his eyes starting to bulge in their sockets. His thick muscle filled arms swelling and straining against the cold hard chains. Every fiber in his body wanted to strike out at the maggot before him, how dare this so-called man of a god try and think that he or his false god was even on the same plain as himself. How could this scum sit here face to face with such an exalted creature such as me and try to beg for my soul, try to make me bow down to a golden calf. Can he not see that I am the only true power in this universe, it can only be through me that these worthless hunks of meat can gain the gift of nothingness, only through my hands can they soar to the heavens of complete and utter emptiness and swim in the vast ocean of self-solitude.

Father Daimen watched in silence as Chris's whole body tightened itself like a spring, he watched as Chris's knuckles turned white, his hands balled into steel like fists, the veins at each side of Chris,s neck threatening to explode sending a double arc of life force jetting across the room. Father Daimen knew that his silence was needed, he had sat with at least 30 other death row inmates over the past 35 years, each in their turn venting the anger and hopelessness through either violence or fear, he understood and sympathized with their plight, his only wish being to help them repent, his calling to save as many souls as he possibly could, his calling only to allow the lord to work through him, his body merely a vessel, a conduit of righteousness, one of faith love and savor.

Like a small child being born, a small grin slowly grew upon Chris,s face. He raised his head slightly as though to give Father Daimen a better view of it. His deep black eyes never leaving the Fathers, two mortal souls locked in a battle for eternity, an endless and ageless fight of good and evil, a timelessly brutal combat of right and wrong.

"You Father fear death just like all the other mindless robots. You cry at night for forgiveness for the fly you swat oR the ant that you inadvertently step upon; I find you and the rest of humanity pathetic. I could stand things no more, I was given this honor of gifting the weak with the prize, me. Me alone was strong enough to show the world its true self, to reach down into the depths of its belly and pull out the rotting feted intestines of life. It was me that showed you all how weak and cattle like you have all become, walking through your lives zombie like, never seeing, never taking hold of the true power which you all hold within your self's. What I did, I did out of pity, out of lust and out of hunger, I feasted upon the bodies of those victims as you call them, I call them my toys."

Father Daimen crossed himself before slowly kissing the golden cross which hung around his neck. "Please my son, go on. You must continue to free yourself of the burden."

"You fool, I have no burden, I carry no regret of false guilt. I am not your son and if I were you Father, I would refrain from saying so again." Chris,s smile retreated back behind its craggy features as he continued. "What I did, what I have begun fulfilled me, it made me whole, with each new kill I became greater than I was before, from my first, the girl which lived above my apartment I grew, even as I dismembered her weak body, I felt the strength growing inside of me. She tasted good, her flesh was sweet and juicy, her muscle fibers strong and tough like steak and her lungs, oh her lungs were a joy to be held, even now I can feel the way each slid down my throat, coated by her blood, her nectre. No Father, from that first one I became the god I am here now. Each new kill, each new toy that I set free fed me in ways you will never understand, ways you can never understand. I am like your Adam standing at the threshold of my Eden looking out and surveying all before me and I see so much to do, so many to free. Each calling out to me, begging me to be their true savor and to set them free, each freely offering their body to me so that I may grow. You see Father this is just the beginning, this is my time of rapture and like all good things I have only just begun, I have to begin, I have to start..."

   Gently everything around Chris began to dissolve, the walls with their oppressive drab grey paint, the yellowing ceiling with its soul sucking fluorescent light, the cold hard metal table, even the unmoving Father Daimen, all slowly disappeared, like a cloudy day begins to brighten it all just faded away and became replaced by a small bathroom, its walls the same drab grey, its yellowing ceiling lit by the same mournful florescent light. Chris no longer held eye contact with Father Daimen, instead he simply stared at himself in the reflection of the broken mirror, its edges dirtied and stained, he sat on the edge of the small filthy bathtub with one crusted tap drip drip dripping, his hands gripping the edge of the sink Infront of the mirror. He steadied himself whilst his mind settled, he knew from bitter experience the vision would return, it had many times over the past several months, he also knew that it was more than just a vision, he knew he had been chosen, knew he had seen things to come...

From above came the all too familiar bursts of angry voices of the Tennent's that lived in the apartment. Their shouts and insults at each other clearly heard below, its sound amplified by the lack of sound deadening which ceased to exist between each apartment.

"This time you can go to hell Jerry. I've put up with enough of your bullshit and I won't take anymore, now get the fuck out, we're through, I'm done." the female outburst was quickly followed with a loud crash like smashing glass, something heavy being thrown swiftly then meeting a fixed object.

A male voice this time but with just as much venom. "Jesus Christ Tracey you could have hit me with that, look you crazy bitch I've tried to explain but if that's how it's going to be fuck you too ill see you round sometime." followed by a loud thud which signaled the slamming of the apartment door.

Still with his gaze fixed upon himself Chris stood, naked to the waist his upper body glistening with perspiration. From above came the sound of crying, soft sobs then small gasps of air quickly taken in before the cycle repeated itself.

Clenching both fists Chris lowered his head a little, "And so it begins." he uttered to himself before leaving his apartment bounding the flight of stairs, he aproached Traceys door to find it slightly ajar. IT BEGINS...

THE END

Printed in Great Britain
by Amazon